The Bat

by
Mary Roberts Rinehart
and Avery Hopwood

A SAMUEL FRENCH ACTING EDITION

SAMUEL FRENCH

FOUNDED 1830

New York Hollywood London Toronto
SAMUELFRENCH.COM

ISBN   978-0-573-60588-8   Printed   in   U.S.A.   #255

DESCRIPTION OF CHARACTERS

MISS CORNELIA VAN GORDER: *An elderly spinster. Act I, opening in evening gown. Change for finish Act I to negligee. Same used throughout the play.*

MISS DALE OGDEN: *A beautiful young girl of twenty-five. Evening gown and cloak. No change.*

LIZZIE ALLEN: *An elderly maid; very eccentric. Act I, opening in a dark, short-sleeved servant's house dress. Change for finish, Act I, to showy kimono. Same used throughout balance of play.*

BILLY: *White washable coat, dark trousers, white shoes.*

ANDERSON: *Dark double-breasted suit.*

RICHARD FLEMING: *Cloth peeked cap, tuxedo coat, white trousers, rain coat.*

BROOKS: *Shabby clothes, blue soft shirt with soft blue collar, a soft cap.*

DOCTOR WELLS: *Dinner coat, First Act. Act II, dark overcoat, dark soft cap. Act III, same as Act I.*

REGINALD BERESFORD: *Dinner clothes, straw hat. No change.*

UNKNOWN MAN: *Old trousers, old shirt, very untidy appearance; old shoes covered with mud.*

MAN *who goes upstairs (in dark), Act I, with wrist watch, dark suit, soft felt hat.*

The following is a copy of program of the first performance of "THE BAT" as produced at the Morosco Theatre,
New York:

Wagenhals & Kemper

Present

"THE BAT"

A Mystery Drama in Three Acts

By MARY ROBERTS RINEHART
and AVERY HOPWOOD

Staged under the direction of
Collin Kemper

CAST OF CHARACTERS

LIZZIE .... *May Vokes*
MISS CORNELIA VAN GORDER .... *Effie Ellsler*
BILLY .... *Harry Morvil*
BROOKS .... *Stuart Sage*
MISS DALE OGDEN .... *Anne Morrison*
DOCTOR WELLS .... *Edward Ellis*
ANDERSON .... *Harrison Hunter*
RICHARD FLEMING .... *Richard Barrows*
REGINALD BERESFORD .... *Kenneth Hunter*
AN UNKNOWN MAN .... *Robert Vaughan*

SYNOPSIS

ACT I. *Living room in Miss Van Gorder's Long
        Island House.*

ACT II. *The same.*

ACT III. *The garret of the same house.*

THE BAT

SCENE: *A combined living room and library of a country house. Open book shelves (four) in the set; one down* R. *below door; one up* R., *above door; one up* C. *in half arch thickness piece; one up* L. *above fireplace. Single door* R. *to front door; dining room. Double doors leading to alcove, small staircase and terrace door, and exit below the stairs and off to the library up* R.C. *All along the back of set,* C. *to* L., *French windows. Six small frames in these windows. Double doors in the* C. *of window to open on stage. Single door up* L.3, *leading to billiard room. Fireplace down* L.

The six small windows in French window effect are fitted with long narrow shades. Light in color. Shades remain down throughout Acts I and II.

Beyond the double doors a small and supplementary staircase, showing stair rail, two steps, newel post (supposed to be newly varnished). Platform and steps carry off R. *Terrace door in the alcove at right angle to the French windows. Thus one enters the house from the terrace past the French windows and the terrace door opens directly on foot of small staircase.*

DISCOVERED: CORNELIA VAN GORDER *and* LIZZIE. CORNELIA *is knitting by the light of the lamp on center table. She is seated in armchair* L. *of*

5

the table. LIZZIE *is at the city telephone up* C. *When Curtain is well up,* LIZZIE *sets down the phone, with angry snap; hangs up the receiver.*

LIZZIE. He says the reason they turned the lights off last night was because there was a storm threatening. He says it burns out their fuses. *(Low rumble of THUNDER in the distance.)* There! They'll be going off again tonight! *(Step* L., *scared.)*

CORNELIA. Humph! I hope it will be a dry summer. Ask Billy to bring some candles and have them ready.

LIZZIE. *(Frightened, moves down to back of table* C.*)* You're not going to ask me to go out into that hall alone?

CORNELIA. *(Putting down knitting)* What's the matter with you, anyhow, Lizzie Allen?

LIZZIE. *(Pleadingly, and shivering with terror)* Oh, Miss Neillie, I don't like it! I want to go back to the city.

CORNELIA. *(Firmly)* I have rented this house for four months, and I am going to stay.

LIZZIE. *(Clutching at* CORNELIA'S *arm)* There's somebody on the terrace!

CORNELIA. *(Also nervous and looking over her shoulder)* Don't do that!

LIZZIE. *(Relieved)* I guess it was the wind.

CORNELIA. *You* were born on a brick pavement. You get nervous out here at night when the crickets begin to sing, or scrape their legs together, or whatever it is they do.

LIZZIE. *(*R.C.*)* Oh, it's more than that, Miss Neillie, I——

CORNELIA. *(Turning to her fiercely)* What did you really see last night?

LIZZIE. I was standing right at the top of that there staircase with your switch in my hand—then I looked down and I saw a gleaming eye. It looked at me and *winked*. I tell you, this house is haunted!

CORNELIA. *(Skeptically)* A flirtatious ghost? Humph! Why didn't you yell?

LIZZIE. I was too scared to yell. And I'm not the only one. Why do you think the servants left all of a sudden? Did you really believe that the house-maid had a pain in her side? Or that the cook's sister had twins? *(Moves slowly up and back of table c. to L.C.)* I bet a cent the cook never had any sister—and her sister never had any twins. *(Down to L.C.)* No, Miss Neillie, they couldn't put it over on me like that. They were scared away. *(Impressively)* They saw—*it*.

CORNELIA. Fiddlesticks! What time is it?

LIZZIE. *(Looks at mantel clock L.)* Half past ten.

CORNELIA. *(Yawns)* Miss Dale won't be home for half an hour. Now you forget that superstitious nonsense! There's nothing in that sort of thing. *(Rolls up her knitting and puts in bag)* Where's that Ouija Board? *(Rises and turns armchair to face L.)*

LIZZIE. *(Shuddering; indicating; points up c.)* It's up there—with a prayer book on it—to keep it quiet.

CORNELIA. Bring it here.

LIZZIE. *(Hesitates; shuddering; protesting in every movement, brings the Ouija Board, carrying it away from her body down to* CORNELIA, L. *of table, carrying board between thumb and forefinger. As she places it in* CORNELIA'S *lap)* You can do it yourself.

CORNELIA. It takes two people, and you know it, Lizzie Allen.

LIZZIE. *(As she speaks, goes up L., gets small chair below door L.3. Comes down with chair. Placing it L. of* CORNELIA*)* I've been working for you for twenty years. I've been your goat for twenty years, and I've got a right to speak my mind.

CORNELIA. You haven't got a mind. Sit down. (LIZZIE *sits.*) Now make your mind a blank.

LIZZIE. *(Frightfully; she and* CORNELIA *put their fingers on Ouija Board)* You just said I haven't got any mind.

CORNELIA. Well, make what you haven't got a blank.

LIZZIE. *(Mumbles)* I've stood by you through thick and thin—I stood by you when you were a Vegetarian—I stood by you when you were a Theosophist—and I seen you through Socialism, Fletcherism and Rheumatism—but when it comes to carrying on with ghosts——

CORNELIA. Be still! Nothing will come if you keep chattering.

LIZZIE. That's *why* I'm chattering! My teeth are, too. I can hardly keep my upper set in. *(She starts)* I've got a queer feeling in my fingers all the way up my arms. *(Wiggles arms.)*

CORNELIA. Hush! *(Pause)* Now, Ouija, is Lizzie Allen right about this house—or is it all stuff and nonsense?

LIZZIE. My Gawd! It's *moving.*

CORNELIA. You shoved it!

LIZZIE. I did not—cross my heart, Miss Neillie, I——

CORNELIA. Keep quiet! *(A moment's pause. Ouija wildly writes, then stops;* CORNELIA *calls off the letters)* B—M—C—X—P—R—S—K—I.

LIZZIE. *(Breathlessly)* Russian! *(Ouija Board continues to move. Pause.)*

CORNELIA. B—A—T—Bat! *(Pause. Ouija stops.* CORNELIA *takes her hands off board)* That's queer.

LIZZIE. *(Turns round, to front)* Bats are un-lucky—everybody knows it. There's been a bat flying around inside this house all evening. *(Rises. Steps back step to* L.*)* Oh, Miss Neillie, please let me sleep in your room tonight. It's only when my jaw drops that I snore. I can tie it up with a handkerchief.

CORNELIA. *(Who is evidently revolving a thought in her mind)* I wish you'd tie it up with a handkerchief now. *(Still thinking. Rises. Puts board on table* C.*)* B—A—T—Bat! Give me the evening paper and my glasses. *(Straightens the armchair to face front, then crosses front of table and sits* R. *of table* C.*)*

LIZZIE. *(Turns, looks around, then sees newspaper on settee. Brings it to* CORNELIA. *Then over* L. *to fireplace, feels mantel over fireplace)* I don't see your glasses here. You'll hurt your eyes reading without 'em. *(Returns* L. *of table.)*

CORNELIA. *(Seated* R.C., *holding newspaper at arm's length. Testily)* My eyes are all right—but my arms aren't long enough. *(She reads)* "Police again baffled by the Bat! *(*LIZZIE *stands* L.C., *scared.)* This unique criminal, known to the underworld as 'The Bat,' has long baffled the Police. The record of his crimes shows him to be endowed with almost diabolical ingenuity. So far there is no clue to his identity—but Anderson, City Detective, today said—'We must cease combing the criminal world for The Bat and look higher. He may be a merchant—a lawyer—a doctor, honored in his community by day—and at night a blood-thirsty assassin.' "

LIZZIE. I'm going to take the butcher knife to bed with me!

CORNELIA. *(Puts hand on Ouija Board)* That thing certainly spelled *Bat!* *(Sits facing front; glances at paper)* I wish I were a *man!* I'd like to see any doctor, lawyer or merchant of my acquaintance lead a double life without my suspecting it! *(Lays down paper on table.)*

LIZZIE. *(Over to chair she brought down earlier)* A man takes to a double life like a woman does to a kimona—it rests him! *(LIZZIE takes up chair; puts it back below door L.3.)*

CORNELIA. *(Knits)* If I had the clues the Police have about that man, I could get him. If I were a detective——

LIZZIE. *(Overcome. Comes down L.C.)* Now it's Detective-ism!

(Enter BILLY R. He is an impassive Jap. Carries tray with small glass pitcher of water, and two glasses. Comes to C.; places tray on table. He starts to exit R. CORNELIA calls him. He stops R.C.)

CORNELIA. Billy. What's all this about the cook's sister not having twins—did she? *(LIZZIE, scared, watching Jap, moves to top of table; pours out two glasses of water: places one for CORNELIA.)*

BILLY. *(Has come down R.C., facing CORNELIA)* Maybe she have twins—— It happen sometime.

CORNELIA. Do you think there was any other reason for her leaving?

BILLY. Maybe!

CORNELIA. *(Knits)* What *was* the reason?

BILLY. All say same thing—house haunted!

CORNELIA. *(Slight laugh)* You know better than that, don't you?

BILLY. *(Shrugs shoulders)* Funny house—find window open—nobody there—door slam—nobody there! *(DOOR SLAM off R. LIZZIE gives a little jump and squeal: steps L. a step. All three look R.)*

CORNELIA. *(Irritably)* Stop that! It was the wind.

BILLY. *(Impassively)* I think not wind.

CORNELIA. *(Look of slight uneasiness. Knitting*

rapidly) How long have you lived in this house?

BILLY. Since Mr. Fleming built.

CORNELIA. And this is the first time you have been disturbed?

BILLY. Last two days only. (LIZZIE *stands* L., *scared.)*

CORNELIA. What about the face you saw last night at the window?

BILLY. Just face—that's all!

CORNELIA. A man's face!

BILLY. Don't know—maybe! It there! It gone!

CORNELIA. Did you go out after it?

BILLY. *(Shakes head)* No, thanks!

LIZZIE. (L.C.) Oh, Miss Neillie—last night when the lights went out I had a token. My oil lamp was full of oil, but do what I would to keep it going, the minute I shut my eyes, out that lamp would go. There ain't a surer token of death! The Bible says, "Let your light shine"—— When a hand you can't see puts your lights out—goodnight! *(There is a moment's silence. Even* CORNELIA *is uncomfortable.)*

CORNELIA. Well, now that you have cheered us up. *(DISTANT ROLL OF THUNDER.* CORNELIA *rises; goes up* R.C. *Pause.)* Bring some candles, Billy, the lights may be going out any moment. (BILLY *starts* R.) And Billy—— (BILLY *stops.)* There's a gentleman arriving on the last train. After he comes you may go to bed. I shall wait up for Miss Dale. *(*BILLY *starts* R.) Oh, and Billy. *(*BILLY *stops.)* See that all the outer doors on this floor are locked and bring the keys here. *(Exit* BILLY R. CORNELIA *works around up stage at* R.C.)

LIZZIE. (L.C.) I know what all this means! I tell you, there's going to be a death sure!

CORNELIA. *(Comes down* R.C.) There certainly will be if you don't keep quiet. Lock the billiard room windows and go to bed. *(Sits R. of table C. Knits.)*

LIZZIE. *(Angry)* I am not going to bed. I am going to pack up and tomorrow I'm going to leave. *(Pause; look)* I asked you on my bended knees not to take this place, two miles from a railroad. For mercy's sake, Miss Neillie, let's go back to the city.

CORNELIA. I am not going. You can make up your mind to that. I'm going to find out what's wrong about this place, if it takes all summer. I came out to the country for a rest, and I'm going to stay and *get* it.

LIZZIE. *(Grimly)* You'll get your Heavenly rest. *(Goes up a little L.)*

CORNELIA. *(Puts knitting away)* Besides—I might as well tell you, Lizzie, I'm having a detective sent down tonight from Police Headquarters, in the city.

LIZZIE. *(Startled, comes down L.C.)* A detective? Miss Neillie, you're keeping something from me! You know something I don't know.

CORNELIA. I hope so. I don't know that I need him—but it will be interesting to watch a good detective's methods. *(She picks up newspaper off table. Reads)* "His last crime was a particularly atrocious one. The body of the murdered man——"

LIZZIE. *(With a wail—quickly to door L.3)* Why don't you read the funny page once in a while? *(Exits quickly L.3, closing door behind her.)*

(LIGHTNING flashes across French windows L.C. CORNELIA reads on to herself, then thinks she hears something; goes into alcove; bolts terrace door: then comes into room and pushes light button up R.C. LIGHTS ALL OUT. THUNDER, distant flashes LIGHTNING. While lights are out, CORNELIA crosses over to French windows, slowly pulls one shade aside

*and looks out. Then she goes back to switch
button; pushes it. LIGHTS FULL UP.)*

BILLY. *(Enters* R. *with three candles and box of
parlor matches. He crosses to small table up* C.;
puts them on table) New gardener come! *(Puts
water glasses on tray, at table* C.)

CORNELIA. *(Up* R.C.) Nice hour for him to get
here! What's his name? *(Takes out knitting.)*

BILLY. Say name Brook.

CORNELIA. Ask him to come in—and Billy—
where are the keys?

BILLY. *(Takes two keys out of pocket; places on
table* C. *Then crosses to* R. *with tray, pitcher and
glasses. As* BILLY *crosses* CORNELIA, *he turns
around and faces her and points up at terrace door)*
Door up there—spring lock. *(Exits* R.2.)

CORNELIA. I know, spring lock.

LIZZIE. *(Enters from billiard room* L.3 *as if she
had been shot out of a gun; leaves door partly open
as she enters. Loud whisper. To* CORNELIA) I
heard somebody yell out in the grounds. Away
down by the gate!

CORNELIA. *(Coming down* R.C.) What did they
yell?

LIZZIE. *(*L.C.) Just yelled a yell!

CORNELIA. *(Crosses front of table and sits chair*
L.C. *Knits)* You take a liver pill and go to bed.
(BILLY *opens door* R.2. *Unseen.* BROOKS *enters.*
BROOKS *is a handsome young fellow, shabbily
dressed, but very neat, and carries a cap in his hand.*
BILLY *closes the door behind him.* BROOKS *is
smooth shaven.)* You are Brooks, the new gar-
dener?

BROOKS. Yes, madam. The butler said you
wanted to speak to me.

CORNELIA. *(Pause. Looks at him)* Come in.
(BROOKS *comes forward two steps. Faces* COR-

NELIA.) You're the man my niece engaged in the city, this afternoon?

BROOKS. Yes, madam.

CORNELIA. *(Knitting)* I could not verify your references, as the Brays are in Canada.

BROOKS. I am sure, if Mrs. Bray *were* here——

CORNELIA. *(Turns in chair; looks at* BROOKS*)* Were here? *(She eyes him with quick suspicion)* Are you a professional gardener?

BROOKS. *(Doubtful)* Yes.

CORNELIA. Know anything about hardy perennials?

BROOKS. Yes, they—they're the ones that keep their leaves during the winter—aren't they?

CORNELIA. Come over here. (BROOKS *steps over to* R.C. CORNELIA *scrutinizes him carefully)* Have you had any experience with rubeola?

BROOKS. Oh, yes—yes—indeed! (LIZZIE *stands; watches* BROOKS. *She is* L.C. *up.)*

CORNELIA. And—alopecia?

BROOKS. The dry weather is very hard on alopecia.

CORNELIA. What do you think is the best treatment for urticaria?

BROOKS. Urticaria frequently needs—er—thinning.

CORNELIA. *(Rises. Faces him across table)* Needs scratching, you mean. Young man, urticaria is hives, rubeola is measles and alopecia is baldness. *(Slight pause. She crosses front of table to* BROOKS *over* R.C. *Suspiciously)* Why did you tell me that you were a professional gardener? Why have you come here at this hour of the night, pretending to be something you are not?

BROOKS. *(Suddenly smiles at her, boyishly)* I know I shouldn't have done it. You'd have found me out anyhow. I don't know *anything* about gardening. The truth is, I was desperate! I *had* to have *work*.

CORNELIA. That's *all*, is it?

BROOKS. That's enough, when you're down and out! *(Turns to front.)*

CORNELIA. *(Somewhat melted)* How do I know you won't steal the spoons?

BROOKS. *(Turns to* CORNELIA. *Lighten up)* Are they *nice* spoons?

CORNELIA. Beautiful spoons.

BROOKS. *(Again engagingly boyish)* Spoons are always a great temptation to me, Miss Van Gorder, but if you'll take me, I'll promise to leave them alone.

CORNELIA. *(With grim humor)* That's *extremely kind* of you. *(She goes to bell up* R.C. *Pushes button.)*

LIZZIE. *(Quickly over and up to* CORNELIA*)* I don't trust him! He's too smooth! (CORNELIA *to window* L.C. LIZZIE *following her, their backs to* BROOKS, *who is* R.C.*)*

CORNELIA. I haven't asked for your opinion, Lizzie.

LIZZIE. You're just as bad as all the rest of 'em. A good looking man comes in the door and your brains fly out the window. *(During this,* BROOKS *has a chance to make a stealthy survey of the room. He does this in such a way that from that time on it is perfectly plain to the audience that his interest in the house is not that of a gardener only.* BROOKS *quickly runs up to alcove* R.C., *looks off and quickly back to* R.C., *so that when* CORNELIA *turns to him, he is where she saw him last.)*

CORNELIA. *(Crosses back to* R.C. *up stage)* Have you had anything to eat lately?

BROOKS. Not since this morning.

(BILLY *enters* R.)

CORNELIA. Billy, give this man something to eat, and then show him where he is to sleep. *(To* BROOKS, *holding out candle and matches. He takes a step up to her.)* Take a candle and a box of matches to your room with you. The local light company crawls under its bed every time there is a thunderstorm. Goodnight, Brooks.

BROOKS. Goodnight, ma'am. *(Over to door* R.) You're being mighty good to me. (CORNELIA *smiles at him as* BROOKS *exits* R. BILLY *exits* R., *closing door.)*

LIZZIE. *(Up* L.C.*)* Haven't you any sense, taking strange men into the house? How do you know that isn't the Bat? *(DISTANT THUNDER, LIGHTS BLINK.)* There go the lights.

CORNELIA. *(Crosses front of table* C. *to* L.C.*)* We'll put the detective in the blue room when he comes. You'd better go up and see if it's all ready. (LIZZIE *lifts newspaper off Ouija, gets board off table* C., *puts prayer book on Ouija and on table up* C. *Then she starts for doors* R.C.*)* Lizzie! (LIZZIE *stops; looks at* CORNELIA.*)* You know that stair rail's just been varnished—use the other stairs. (LIZZIE *starts for door* R.2*)*—and Lizzie——

LIZZIE. Yes'm.

CORNELIA. No one is to know that he is a detective—not even Billy.

LIZZIE. What'll I *say* he is?

CORNELIA. *(Sits* L.C. *at table)* It's nobody business.

(DOORBELL off R.*)*

LIZZIE. *(Near door* R.*)* A detective! Tiptoeing around with his eyes to all the keyholes. A body won't be safe in the bathtub—— *(Exits* R. *Pause.* CORNELIA *turns and looks at door* R.*)*

(Enter BILLY R.*)*

BILLY. *(As he comes and goes to table* C. *for key)* Front door key, please.

CORNELIA. Find out who it is before you unlock the door. (BILLY *gets key off table* C. *and exits* R., *leaving door open.* CORNELIA *rises; looks toward door* R.*)*

DALE. *(Off* R.*)* Won't you come in for a few minutes?

DOCTOR. *(Off* R.*)* Oh, thank you. *(*CORNELIA *sits with knitting,* L.C.*)*

(Enter DALE OGDEN R. *She is a beautiful young girl of twenty-two. She wears a pale-colored charming evening frock and evening wrap. She enters quietly and without animation.)*

CORNELIA. Aren't you back early, Dale?

DALE. *(To chair above door* R., *throws off her wrap)* I was tired——

CORNELIA. Not worried about anything?

DALE. *(Comes down* R.C. *to chair* R. *of table* C. *Sits. Unconvincingly)* No, but I've come out here to be company for you, and I don't want to run away all the time.

DOCTOR. *(Off* R.*)* How have you been, Billy?

BILLY. *(Off* R.*)* Very well, thanks.

CORNELIA. Who's out there, Dale?

DALE. Doctor Wells—he brought me over from the club. I asked him to come in for a few minutes —Billy's just taking his coat.

CORNELIA. Your trunks have come.

DALE. *(Listlessly)* That's good. *(Rises and turns; goes up back of table.)*

CORNELIA. I hope this country air will pick you up. I promised your mother before she sailed that I'd take good care of you. (DALE *leans over; kisses* CORNELIA. *Then* DALE *goes* L.C. *Sits settee, which is up and down stage* L.C. *Faces fireplace.)*

(DOCTOR WELLS *enters* R. *He is in dinner clothes; good looking man in his early forties—with a shrewd, rather acquiline face.* BILLY *enters* R., *goes to top of table* C., *puts key on table, then exits* R.; *closes door.*)

DOCTOR. *(Crosses to table* R.C.; *shakes hands with* CORNELIA*)* Well, how are we this evening. Miss Van Gorder?

CORNELIA. Very well, thank you, Doctor. Well, many people at the Country Club?

DOCTOR. Not very many. This failure of the Union Bank has knocked a good many of the club members sky high.

CORNELIA. Just how did it happen?

DOCTOR. Oh, the usual thing. The cashier, a young chap named Bailey, looted the bank to the tune of over a million. (CORNELIA *surprised.*)

DALE. *(Visibly agitated)* How do you *know* the cashier did it?

DOCTOR. Well, he's run away, for one thing. The Bank Examiner found the deficit this morning. Bailey, the cashier, went out for lunch and didn't come back. The method was simple—blank paper substituted for securities.

DALE. Couldn't somebody else have done it? (CORNELIA *looks at* DALE, *then at* DOCTOR.*)

DOCTOR. Of course the President of the bank had access to the vaults. But as you know, Mr. Courtleigh Fleming, the late President, was buried last Monday.

CORNELIA. Dale dear, did you know this young Bailey?

DALE. *(Controlling herself with an effort)* Yes —slightly.

CORNELIA. What with bank robberies and Bolshevism and the Income Tax, the only way to keep your money these days is to spend it.

DOCTOR. *(Sits R.C. at table)* Or *not* to *have* any! Like myself!

CORNELIA. You know, Dale, this is Courtleigh Fleming's house. I rented it from his nephew only last week.

DOCTOR. As a matter of fact, Dick Fleming had no right to rent you this property before the estate was settled. He must have done it the moment he received my telegram announcing his uncle's death.

CORNELIA. Were you with him when he died?

DOCTOR. Yes—— In Colorado—— It was very sudden.

CORNELIA. *(Knitting and in an innocent tone)* I suppose there is no suspicion that Courtleigh Fleming robbed his own bank?

DOCTOR. Well, if he did—I can testify he didn't have the loot with him. No, he had his faults—but not that.

CORNELIA. Doctor, I think I ought to tell you something. Last night and the night before, attempts were made to enter this house. Once an intruder actually got in, and was frightened away by Lizzie, at the top of that staircase. *(Indicating rear.)* And twice I have received anonymous communications threatening my life if I did not leave this house.

DALE. *(Startled)* I didn't know that, Auntie. How dreadful!

CORNELIA. Don't tell Lizzie. She'd yell like a siren. It's the only thing she can do like a siren, but she does it superbly. *(At this moment, pane of one of the French windows up L.C. is smashed in, and a stone with a note tied to it with a piece of string is thrown into the room. ALL rise quickly and look up at windows.)*

DALE. What's that?

CORNELIA. Somebody smashed a window pane.

DALE. And threw in a stone.

DOCTOR. Wait a minute. I'll—— *(He hurries up to alcove and terrace door.)*

CORNELIA. *(Follows up a few steps* R.C.*)* It's bolted at the top. *(DOCTOR unbolts door leading to terrace, and goes out; passes French windows to* L. *Meanwhile,* DALE *has gone up* L.C., *picked up stone, comes down* L.C., *unties string off stone, hands note to* CORNELIA *after she has closed terrace door.* DALE *drops stone on settee.* CORNELIA *to top of table, unfolds the note and reads it)* "Take warning. Leave this house at once! It is threatened with disaster, which will involve you if you remain."

DALE. *(*L. *of* CORNELIA*)* Who do you think wrote it?

CORNELIA. A fool, that's who! If anything was calculated to make me remain here, this sort of thing would do it. *(Slaps paper.)*

DALE. But—something may happen.

CORNELIA. *(Comes down* R.C.*)* I hope so! That's the reason I——

(DOORBELL rings off R.*)*

DALE. *(Startled)* Oh, don't let anyone in. *(Down a step below* CORNELIA.*)*

BILLY. *(Enters* R. *Crosses to table* C., *gets key before he speaks)* Key front door, please; bell ring.

CORNELIA. *(Crosses front of table to* R.C.*)* See that the chain is on the door. And get the visitor's name before you admit him. *(Crosses to* BILLY*)* If he gives the name Anderson, let him in and take him to the library. *(*BILLY *exits* R.; *closes door.)*

DALE. *(*L.C.*)* Anderson—— Who is——

CORNELIA. *(Pause; thinks; to* C., *front of table)* Dale dear—perhaps you had better go back to the city.

DALE. *(Surprised)* Tonight?

CORNELIA. *(Impassively)* There is something behind all this disturbance—something I don't understand. But I mean to. *(Looks* R. *and up to see if* DOCTOR's *returning, then moves step* L., *close to* DALE. *Lowers voice)* The man in the library is a detective from Police Headquarters.

DALE. *(Unacccuntably aghast)* Not—the Police.

CORNELIA. Sh—— Be careful. *(Steps to* R.; *then back to* DALE*)* It's not necessary to tell the *Doctor.* I think *he's* a sort of perambulating bedside gossip. *(Slight pause)* If it's *known* that the police are here, we'll *never* catch the criminals.

(DOCTOR *enters terrace door; comes down* R.C., *trifle out of breath. Takes out handkerchief; shakes off rain.)*

DOCTOR. He got away in the shrubbery.

CORNELIA. *(Steps from front of table to* DOCTOR; *hands him note)* Read this. (DALE *sits settee* L.; *stares front, clearly terrified.)*

DOCTOR. *(Up* R.C.; *reads, pauses, then looks at* CORNELIA*)* Were the others like this?

CORNELIA. Practically. *(Crosses to* L., *front table.)*

DOCTOR. Miss Van Gorder, may I speak frankly? *(Comes down.)*

CORNELIA. Generally speaking, I detest frankness.

DOCTOR. *(Still* R.C.*)* I think you *ought* to leave this house.

CORNELIA. *(Takes it lightly)* Because of that letter?

DOCTOR. *(Seriously)* There is some deviltry afoot. You are not safe here.

CORNELIA. I have been safe in all kinds of houses for sixty years. It's time I had a bit of a change. *(Starts up* L.C. *as she speaks)* Besides, this house is as nearly impregnable as I can make it. *(She faces the French windows up* L.C.*)* The window locks are sound—the doors are locked and the keys are here. *(Steps to back of table* c.; *points to keys on table)* On that door to the terrace—*(Looks up* R.C.*)*—I had Billy today place an extra bolt. By the way, did you bolt that door again? *(She is about to go up to terrace door.* DOCTOR *takes a step up to stop her.)*

DOCTOR. Yes, I did. (CORNELIA *stops.)* Miss Van Gorder, I confess I'm very anxious for you. This letter is ominous. Have you any enemies?

CORNELIA. Don't insult me! Of course I have. Enemies are an indication of character.

DOCTOR. Why not accept my hospitality in the villiage tonight. It's a little house, but I'll make you comfortable. Or, if you won't come, let *me* stay *here.*

CORNELIA. Thank you, no, Doctor, I'm not easily frightened. (DOCTOR *looks at letter.)* And to-morrow I intend to equip this entire house with burglar alarms on doors and windows. *(She goes up into alcove and to terrace door; pushes bolt)* I knew it. *(Triumphantly)* Doctor, you *didn't* fasten that bolt!

DOCTOR. *(*R.C., *facing up stage)* Oh, I'm sorry—

CORNELIA. You pushed it only part of the way. *(Sees door is bolted, comes down, crosses above table to* L.C.*)* The only thing that worries me now is that broken window. Anyone can reach a hand through it and open the latch. *(She goes down* L. *to settee.* DALE *rises, and stands well down* L.; *faces up to see what* CORNELIA *intends to do.)* Please, Doctor!

DOCTOR. What do you mean to do?

CORNELIA. I'm going to barricade that window. (DOCTOR *comes over above table* C. *and down* L.C. *to end of settee, facing down stage.* DALE *makes gesture to* CORNELIA *to stand aside.* CORNELIA *takes a step back towards fireplace.* DOCTOR *and* DALE *push up settee* L.C. *until it is against* C. *of French windows.)*

DOCTOR. It would take a furniture mover to get in there now.

CORNELIA. *(Comes up* L.C. DALE *goes down* L.) Well, Doctor, now I'll say goodnight—and thank you very much. *(Crosses above table to* R.C.; *then turns; faces* DOCTOR, *who is up* C.) Don't keep this young lady up too late—she looks tired.

DOCTOR. I'll only smoke a cigarette. You won't change your mind?

CORNELIA. *(Smiles)* I've got a great deal of mind. It takes a long time to change it. *(She exits* R.; *closes door.)*

DOCTOR. *(Rather nettled)* It may be mind—but —forgive me if I say I think it is foolhardy stubborness.

DALE. *(Steps over and up* L.C.) Then you think there is really danger?

DOCTOR. *(Up above table* C.) Well, those letters —*(He has placed it on table)*—mean *something*—— Here you are—isolated—the village two miles away—and enough shrubbery around the place to hide a dozen assassins.

DALE. But what enemies can she have?

DOCTOR. *(Takes cigarette from case. Step to* C.) Any man will tell you what I do. This is no place for two women, practically alone. (DALE *walks away to fireplace; back to* DOCTOR. *Unseen by her, he steps down* R. *of table, takes match box off match holder and slips it into his side pocket. Then with assumed carelessness)* I don't seem to see any matches. *(Looks up at stand* C.)

DALE. *(Turns; faces him)* Oh, aren't there any? I'll get you some. (DALE *quickly crosses front of table and exits* R.; *closes door.* DOCTOR *watches her off, then swiftly he runs up into alcove* R.C., *unfastens bolt on terrace door. He quickly comes back to same position top of table up* C., *picks up a book and opens it. Enter* DALE R. *with matches. She crosses to him; gives him matches.)*

DOCTOR. I'm so sorry to trouble you—but tobacco is the one drug every doctor forbids his patients and prescribes for himself. (DALE *smiles at his little joke. Then she crosses front of table to* L.C. DOCTOR *works around table and down to* R.C. *Lights cigarette)* By the way, has Miss Van Gorder a revolver?

DALE. *(Turns; faces him)* Yes, she fired it off this evening to see if it would work.

DOCTOR. If she tries to shoot at anything, for goodness' sake stand behind her. Oh, I must be going. *(Starts to go* R.; *looks at wrist watch.)*

DALE. If anything happens, I shall *telephone* you at once.

DOCTOR. *(Stops on word "telephone," hesitates; then)* I'll be home shortly after midnight. I'm stoping at the Johnsons'. One of the children is ill. *(A step to* R., *then turns back; faces* DALE) Take a parting word of advice. The thing to do with a midnight prowler is—let him alone. Lock your bedroom doors, and don't let anything bring you out until morning. *(Goes to door.)*

DALE. Thank you. Billy will let you out. He has the key.

DOCTOR. *(At door* R.) By jove, *you're* careful, aren't you? *(Looks around)* The place is like a fortress! Well, goodnight, Miss Dale.

DALE. Goodnight. *(Exit* R., DOCTOR. *Pause. DOOR SLAM off* R. DALE *is left alone. Stands motionless, takes out handkerchief, dabs eyes. She is distressed for some unknown reason. Crosses to fireplace.* BILLY *counts five, then enters* R., *puts door key on table* C. DALE *picks up book)* Billy, has the new gardener come?

BILLY. He here—name Brook. *(Exit* BILLY R.,

leaving door open. Stands in sight while they enter.
CORNELIA *sweeps in, followed by* ANDERSON. *He is
a man of probably fifty, an aggressive person with a
loud voice. Not at all the typical stage detective.)*

CORNELIA. Dale, dear, this is Mr. Anderson.

DETECTIVE. *(To* R.C.*)* How do you do? (DALE
bows; does not speak.)

CORNELIA. *(Up* R.*)* This is the room I spoke of.
All the disturbances have taken place around that
door. *(Indicating terrace door.)*

DETECTIVE. *(Up to alcove)* This is not the main
staircase?

CORNELIA. No, the main staircase is out there.
(Indicating R.*)*

DETECTIVE. *(*R.C. *Looking over at French windows)* I think there must be a conspiracy between
architects and the House Breakers Union these
days. Look at all that glass. All a burglar needs is
a piece of putty and a diamond cutter to break in.

CORNELIA. But the curious thing is that whoever
got into the house evidently had a key to that door.
(Indicating terrace door.)

DETECTIVE. Hello—what's that? *(Sees broken
glass on floor up* L.C. *in front of settee. He crosses
up and over to window.* CORNELIA *comes down to*
R. *of table, and faces up, watching* DETECTIVE.
DETECTIVE *picks up piece of glass off floor front of
settee. Places glass on settee.)*

DALE. *(Over* L.*)* It was broken from the outside, a few minutes ago. (DETECTIVE *pulls aside
one of the blinds; looks out.)*

DETECTIVE. The outside?

DALE. And then that letter was thrown in.
(Points to C. *table.* DETECTIVE *comes down to top
of table* C. CORNELIA *hands him the note that was
thrown in.* DETECTIVE *pauses; looks at letter.)*

DETECTIVE. *(Calm; self-assured)* Um! Coy,
isn't it? Somebody wants you *out* of here, all right!

CORNELIA. *(Facing him across table. She is* R. *of table* C.*)* There are some things I haven't told you yet. This house belonged to the late Courtleigh Fleming.

DETECTIVE. *(With interest)* The Union Bank?

CORNELIA. Yes. I rented it for the summer and moved in last Monday. I have not had a really quiet night since I came. The very first night I saw a man with an electric flashlight making his way through that shrubbery. *(Points.* DETECTIVE *is looking up at window.)*

DALE. You poor dear! And you were here alone!

CORNELIA. Well, I had Lizzie. *(She opens drawer* R. *side of table* C. *Takes out a small revolver)* —and I had a revolver. I know so little about these things that if I didn't hit a burglar I'd certainly hit *somebody* or something. *(Looks into the barrel; then waves it about carelessly.)*

DETECTIVE. *(Turns; faces* CORNELIA. *Sees revolver. Starts)* Would you mind putting that away? I like to get in the papers as much as anybody, but I don't want to have them say *"omit* flowers." *(*CORNELIA *replaces revolver in drawer; closes it.* DETECTIVE *goes* R. *and up, facing doors* R.C.*)* Now, you say, you don't think anybody has got upstairs yet?

CORNELIA. *(Moves around front of table to* L.C., *turns, looks up* R.C.*)* I think not. I'm a very light sleeper, especially since the papers have been so full of the exploits of this criminal they call "The Bat." I was just reading your statement about him in the evening paper. *(Sits* L. *of table.)*

DETECTIVE. *(Comes down* R.C., *professional manner)* Yes. He's contrived to surround himself with such an air of mystery that it verges on the supernatural. *(*DALE *sits* L. DETECTIVE *looks* R.*)*

CORNELIA. I confess I have thought of him in *this* connection. *(*DETECTIVE *laughs.)* Nevertheless,

somebody has been trying to get into this house—
night after night.

DETECTIVE. *(Looks around. Seriously)* Any
liquor stored here?

CORNELIA. Yes.

DETECTIVE. *(Interested)* What?

CORNELIA. *(With pride; knits)* Eleven bottles of
home-made elderberry wine.

DETECTIVE. You're safe. *(To table* c.; *looks
newspaper. Shakes head)* You can always tell when
The Bat has anything to do with a crime. When
he's through he signs his name to it. *(Sits; plays
with box of matches.)*

CORNELIA. His name? I thought nobody knew
his name.

DETECTIVE. That was a figure of speech. The
newspapers named him "The Bat" because he moved
with incredible rapidity—always at night—and he
seemed to be able to see in the dark.

CORNELIA. I wish I could. These country lights
are always going out.

DETECTIVE. Within the last six months he's taken
up the name himself—pure bravado——- Sometimes
he draws the outline of a bat, at the scene of the
crime. Once, in some way, he got hold of a real
bat and nailed it to the wall. *(Shudder from* DALE
and CORNELIA.) He seems to have imagination.
(Slaps knee, rises, takes step R. *determinedly)* I've
got imagination, too. *(Stands second, then with effort brings himself back to present situation)* How
many people in this house, Miss Van Gorder? (DALE
starts to cross to R. *above table. She does this
slowly.)*

CORNELIA. My niece and myself; Lizzie Allen,
who has been my personal maid for twenty years—
the Japanese butler and the gardener. The cook,
parlor maid and house maid left yesterday—frightened away. *(Smiles.* DALE *picks up her wrap on*

chair above door R. *and exits* R. DETECTIVE *just glances at her as she goes.)*

DETECTIVE. Well, you can have a good night's sleep tonight. I'll stay right here in the dark and watch.

CORNELIA. Would you like some coffee to keep you awake?

DETECTIVE. Thank you. Do the servants know who I am? *(Cross to* R. *of table.)*

CORNELIA. Only Lizzie—my maid.

DETECTIVE. I wouldn't tell anyone that I am remaining up all night.

CORNELIA. You don't suspect my household?

DETECTIVE. I'm not taking any chances.

LIZZIE. *(Enters* R.; *stands at door)* The gentleman's room is ready.

CORNELIA. *(Knitting;* L.C. *at table)* The maid will show you your room now, and you can make yourself *comfortable* for the night.

DETECTIVE. *(Facing up stage)* My toilet is made for an occasion like this when I've got my gun loaded. (LIZZIE *gives a start. His hand on hip pocket.* DETECTIVE *stares at* LIZZIE, *and goes over* R. *to her)* This is the maid you referred to? (LIZZIE *stiffens.)* What's your name?

LIZZIE. Elizabeth Allen.

DETECTIVE. How old are you? (LIZZIE *looks across at* CORNELIA.)

LIZZIE. Have I got to answer that? (CORNELIA *nods her head. Cute-like)* Thirty-two.

CORNELIA. She's forty. (LIZZIE *gives a start.)*

DETECTIVE. Now, Lizzie, do you ever walk in your sleep?

LIZZIE. I do not.

DETECTIVE. Don't care for the country, I suppose?

LIZZIE. I do not.

DETECTIVE. *(Facetiously)* Or detectives?

LIZZIE. *I do not.*

DETECTIVE. All right, Lizzie. Be calm! I can stand it! *(He goes to table* C., *picks up note that was thrown through window, crosses back beside* LIZZIE, *holds out note so* LIZZIE *can read it. Quick)* Ever see this before?

LIZZIE. *(Reads it; is horrified. Makes gesture with arm, nearly hitting* DETECTIVE *in face)* Mercy on us!

DETECTIVE. *(Watching her)* Didn't write it yourself, did you?

LIZZIE. *(Angrily)* I did *not*!

DETECTIVE. You're sure you don't walk in your sleep?

LIZZIE. *(Strong)* When I get into bed in this house I wouldn't put my feet out for a million dollars.

DETECTIVE. Well, that's more money than I'm worth.

LIZZIE. Well, *I'll say it is. (She flounces out* R.; *slams door behind her.* CORNELIA *laughs.)*

DETECTIVE. *(Turns and goes* R.C. *to table; puts note back on table)* Now, what about the *butler?*

CORNELIA. Nothing about him—except that he was Courtleigh Fleming's servant.

DETECTIVE. Do you consider that significant?

*(*DALE *enters from below stair alcove up* R.C. *Stands watching and listening to* DETECTIVE.*)*

CORNELIA. Is it not possible that there is a connection between this colossal theft at the Union Bank and *these* disturbances?

DETECTIVE. *(Looks at* DALE. *Pause)* Just what do you mean? *(*DALE *slowly moves to* L. *above table* C.*)*

CORNELIA. Suppose Courtleigh Fleming took

that money from his own bank and concealed it in this house?

DETECTIVE. That's the theory you gave Headquarters, isn't it? But I'll tell you how Headquarters figures it out. In the first place, the cashier is missing. In the second place, if Courtleigh Fleming did it, and got as far as Colorado, he'd have had it with him. In the third place, suppose he had hidden the money in or around this house. Why did he rent it to you? (DALE *is over* L. *by this time.*)

CORNELIA. But he didn't. I leased this house from his nephew—his heir.

DETECTIVE. Well, I wouldn't struggle like that for a theory. The cashier's *missing*—that's the answer.

CORNELIA. *(Resents, with pride)* I've read a great deal on the detection of crime, and——

DETECTIVE. *(Interrupting her)* Huh! I suppose so—there are a lot of amateur detectives crawling around over the country today, measuring foot prints with a tape measure. Much as your life's worth to leave a thumb print on a soda water glass. The only real detectives outside the profession are married women. *(Two steps up.)*

CORNELIA. Then *you* don't think there's a chance that the money from the Union Bank is in this house? *(Puts knitting away.)*

DETECTIVE. Very unlikely!

CORNELIA. *(Rises)* If you come with me, I'll show you to your room. *(She crosses front of table to* R. DETECTIVE *steps back to let her pass, then follows her towards door* R.)

DETECTIVE. Well, I suppose I might as well see where I park my tooth brush.

(CORNELIA *exits* R., *followed by* DETECTIVE. DALE *is now seen to be in a state of violent excitement. She goes to door* R.; *then to door* R.C.;

quick to c. *Door* R.C. *opens cautiously.* BROOKS
enters.)

DALE. Sh! Sh! Be careful! That man's a
detective! (BROOKS *looks quickly off* R.C., *then
closes door, and goes to* c., *front of table.* DALE
follows him over.)

BROOKS. Then they've traced me here?

DALE. I don't think so.

BROOKS. I couldn't get back to my rooms. If
they've searched them—*(Pause)*—as they're sure
to—they'll find your letters to me. *(Pause)* Your
aunt doesn't suspect anything?

DALE. No, I told her I'd engaged a gardener—
and that's all there was about it.

BROOKS. Dale! *(Steps* L., *then turns and faces*
DALE R.C.) You *know* I didn't take that money.

DALE. Of course! I believe in you absolutely.

BROOKS. *(He catches her in his arms, kisses her,
then breaks and holds* DALE'S *hands. Steps* L.C.;
drops DALE'S *hands)* But—the Police here—what
does that mean?

DALE. Aunt Cornelia says people have been trying to break into this house for a week—at night.

BROOKS. *(Sharply)* What sort of people? *(Steps
back.)*

DALE. She doesn't know.

BROOKS. *(A step to* L.C.) That proves exactly
what I have contended right along. *(Turns; looks at*
DALE) Courtleigh Fleming took that money and
put it here. And somebody knows that he did.

DALE. The detective thinks you're guilty because
you ran away.

BROOKS. Ran away? *(Turns front; smiles)* The
only chance I had was a few hours to myself, to try
to prove what actually happened. *(Cross* L. *two
steps.)*

DALE. Why don't you tell the detective what you

think? That Courtleigh Fleming took the money, and that it's still here?

BROOKS. He'd take me into custody at once— *(Looks* L.*)*—and I'd have no chance to search. *(Crosses up* L.C.*)*

DALE. Why are you so *sure* it is here?

BROOKS. *(Crosses to* DALE*)* You must remember, Fleming was no ordinary defaulter—and *he* had no intentiou of being exiled to a foreign country. He wanted to come back here and take his place in the community while I was in the Pen.

DALE. But even then——

BROOKS. *(Interrupting)* Listen, dear. (DALE *up to* R.C. *when* BROOKS *goes up to door* L.3, *closing it; comes down slowly to* L.C. *Quietly)* The architect who built this house was an old friend of mine. We were together in France and you know the way fellows get to talking when they're far away. (BROOKS *comes down* L.C.*)* Just an hour or two before a shell got him, he told me he had built a *hidden room* in this house.

DALE. *(Pauses. Looks up* R.*; then speaks)* Where? *(Below table.)*

BROOKS. *(Crosses below table)* I don't know. We never got to finish that conversation. But I remember what he said—— *(Face front)* He said "You watch old Fleming. If I get mine over here, it won't break his heart." He didn't want any living being to know about that room.

DALE. *(Excitedly; whisper)* Then you think the money is in this hidden room?

BROOKS. I do. I don't think Fleming took it West with him. He knew the minute this thing blew up he'd be under suspicion. *(Looks* L.*)* Only if he left the money here, why did he rent this house?

DALE. He didn't. His *nephew* rented it to us. *(Pause. She takes a step* R. *Looks and then back to* C. *and crosses to* BROOKS) Jack, could it be the nephew who's trying to break in?

BROOKS. He wouldn't *have* to break in. He could make an excuse and come at any time. *(Goes over* L.; *looks around)* If I could only get hold of a blueprint of this place.

DALE. *(Crossing front of table.* BROOKS *to fireplace.)* Oh, Jack, I'm so confused and worried!

BROOKS. *(He stops her; hands on shoulders in effort to cheer her. Pause.)* Now, listen—this isn't as hard as it sounds. I've got a clear night to work in—and as true as I'm standing here, that money's in the house. Now listen, honey, it's like this. *(Pantomime action of house on floor)* Here's the house that Courtleigh Fleming built—here, somewhere, is the Hidden Room in the house that Courtleigh Fleming built—and here, somewhere—pray Heaven—is the money, in the Hidden Room, in the house that Courtleigh Fleming built! When you're low in your mind, just say that over!

DALE. *(Smiles faintly)* I've forgotten it already!

BROOKS. *(Still trying to cheer her)* Why, look here! *(Hands on her shoulders, turns her around so she faces front. He goes down stage in front of her. His back to audience)* It's a sort of game, dearest—"Money, money, who's got the money." You know. *(Looks around room)* For that matter, the Hidden Room may be behind these very walls. *(*BROOKS *sees golf sticks in bag leaning against small table up* C.; *quickly up and gets one club. Comes down to fireplace.* DALE *watches him; gives way to* L.C. BROOKS *taps wall above fireplace. ROLL OF THUNDER. LIGHTS BLINK. LIGHTNING.)*

DALE. The lights are going out again.

BROOKS. Let them go. The less light the better for me. The only thing to do is to go over this house room by room. *(Indicates door* L.3*)* What's in there?

Dale. The billiard room. (Brooks *starts as if to exit* L.3.) Jack! Perhaps Courtleigh Fleming's nephew would know where the blueprints are!

Brooks. It's a chance, but not a very good one. *(Exit* Brooks *and* Dale *into* L.3, *leaving door open.)*

(Brooks *RAPS with golf club on ladder off* L. *Pause, then RAPS again. Enter* Lizzie R. *with white table napkin. As soon as she gets inside, LIGHTS BLINK quickly several times.* Lizzie *looks nervously about. THUNDER. LIGHTNING. She shows she is scared; to table with napkin; spreads it on upper end of table.* Brooks *repeats RAPS.* Lizzie *starting for* R., *looking back.)*

Lizzie. Spirits! *(Over to door* R.*)* Go back to Hell, where you *started* from. *(Exits* R. *LIGHTS OUT. LIGHTNING and THUNDER STOP. Enter* Brooks *and* Dale.*)*

Brooks. Well, here we are, back where we started from.

Dale. *(To* C. *up stage)* There's a candle on the table, if I can find the table. Here it is. *(Finds candle on table up* C.*)*

Brooks. (L. *of* Dale) I have matches. *(He lights candle. LIGHTS come up in second strip in foots and second ray light in border. One candle effect. Places candle on table* C.*)* It's pretty nearly hopeless. If all the walls are panelled like that. *(RAPPINGS heard overhead—four dull raps.)*

Dale. *(Suddenly interrupting; backs* R.*)* What's that?

Brooks. *(In tense voice and looking up at ceiling)* Some one else is looking for the Hidden Room. *(Four dull RAPS heard again.)*

Dale. *(Looking up at ceiling, steps toward* C.*)* Upstairs!

BROOKS. Who's in this house besides ourselves?

DALE. Only the detective—Aunt Cornelia—Lizzie and Billy.

BROOKS. Billy's the Jap?

DALE. Yes.

BROOKS. Belong to your aunt?

DALE. No, he was Courtleigh Fleming's butler. *(Four RAPS upstairs.)*

BROOKS. *(Looks up at ceiling)* He was, eh? *(Quickly puts down candle; crosses to doors* R.C. *and into alcove)* It may be the Jap. *(Four more RAPS upstairs.)* If it is, I'll get him. (BROOKS *exits* R.C. *quickly but quietly. Closes door behind him.* DALE, *left alone, stands thinking. Her distress and anxiety are evident. Crosses to* L.C. *At last she forms a resolution. Goes up to city phone.)*

DALE. *(At phone)* One-two-four. *(She looks around before calling number, her voice is cautious)* Is that the Country Club? Is Mr. Richard Fleming there? Yes—I'll hold the wire. *(Moment's pause. She looks around nervously)* Hello—— Is this Mr. Fleming?—This is Miss Ogden.—Do you remember my aunt has rented your house, Cedarcrest? I know it's rather odd my calling you so late, but—I wonder if you could come over here for a few minutes. Yes—tonight. I wouldn't trouble you but—it's awfully important. Hold the wire a moment. *(She puts the receiver down; glances up the stairs; goes* R., *listens at door, then back again to phone)* Hello. I shall wait outside the house on the drive. It—it's a confidential matter.—Thank you so much. *(She hangs up phone; goes* L. *A moment's pause, then* DETECTIVE *enters* R. *with unlighted candle in his hand.)*

DETECTIVE. *(Coming* C.*)* Spooky sort of place in the dark, isn't it?

DALE. *(To chair down* L.C.*)* Yes—rather!

DETECTIVE. *(*R.C.*)* Left me upstairs without a

match. I found my way down by walking part of the way and falling the rest. I don't suppose I'll ever find the room I left my toothbrush in! *(Lights his candle from the lighted candle on* C. *table. LIGHTS come up in sections, foots and border. Two candle light.)*

DALE. You're not going to stay up all night, are you?

DETECTIVE. *(Above* C. *table; takes cigar out)* Oh, I may doze a bit. What's your opinion of these intrusions your aunt complains of?

DALE. I don't know. I only came today.

DETECTIVE. *(Moves little* L.*)* Is she a pretty nervous temperament usually? Imagines she sees things and all that?

DALE. *(Steps down* L.*)* I don't think so.

DETECTIVE. *(*L.C.*)* Know the Flemings?

DALE. I've met Mr. Richard Fleming once or twice.

DETECTIVE. *(Turns to table)* Know the cashier of the Union Bank?

DALE. *(After a barely perceptible pause)* No. *(Moves to fireplace.)*

DETECTIVE. Fellow of good family, I understand —very popular. That's what's behind most of these bank embezzlements. Men getting into society and spending more than they make. *(PHONE up* C. *rings.* DETECTIVE *starts for house phone up* R. *above door.)*

DALE. No, the other one; that's the house phone.

DETECTIVE. *(Looking at house phone)* No connection with the outside, eh?

DALE. No, just from room to room, in the house.

DETECTIVE. *(Goes to phone up* C.*)* Hello! Hello! *(Pause. Hangs up phone)* This line sounds dead.

DALE. It was all right a few minutes ago. *(Sits down* L.*)*

DETECTIVE. You were using it a few minutes ago?

DALE. *(Hesitates, then)* Yes. *(PHONE up* c. *rings again.)*

DETECTIVE. *(Picks up phone)* Yes, yes—*this* is Anderson—go ahead—— *(Rather impatiently)* You're sure of that—are you?—I see—— All right! 'Bye! *(Hangs up phone; turns and looks at* DALE *intently)* Did I understand you to say that you are not acquainted with the cashier of the Union Bank? *(Down to back of table* c. *Pause.* DALE *stares ahead; does not reply.)* That was Headquarters, Miss Ogden. They have found some letters in Bailey's room which seem to indicate that you were not telling the entire truth just now.

DALE. What letters?

DETECTIVE. From you to Jack Bailey—showing that you had recently become engaged to him.

DALE. Very well. That's true.

DETECTIVE. Why didn't you say so before?

DALE. *(Frankly)* It's been a secret. I haven't even told my aunt yet. *(Rises)* How can the Police be so stupid as to accuse Jack Bailey—a young man about to be married? Do you think he would wreck his future like that?

DETECTIVE. Well, some folks wouldn't call it wrecking a future to lay away a million dollars. *(To* L.C. *Speaks slowly and ominously)* Do you know *where* he is now?

DALE. No.

DETECTIVE. Miss Ogden, in the last minute or so the Union Bank case and certain things in this house begin to tie up pretty close together. *(Steps a little nearer to her* L.*)* Bailey disappeared at three o'clock this afternoon. Have you heard from him since then?

DALE. No.

DETECTIVE. You used the telephone a few minutes ago. Did you *call* him?

DALE. No.

DETECTIVE. I'll ask you to bring Miss Van Gorder here.

DALE. Why do you want her?

DETECTIVE. Because this case is taking on a new phase.

DALE. You don't think I know anything about that money?

DETECTIVE. No, but you know—somebody who does.

(DALE *hesitates, about to reply, then finding none, goes* R. *front of table, taking a lighted candle with her. Gets it off* C. *table. Exits* R. *LIGHTS down to one candle effect.* DETECTIVE, *left alone, reflects for a moment, then he picks up lighted candle from table* C.; *proceeds to make a systematic examination of walls. ELECTRICIAN watch him as he goes up into alcove. Follow to* R. *in foots. Dim away down as he goes into alcove. Catch him as he comes out of alcove and crosses to* L. *Follow candle until he exits* L.3. *LIGHTS OUT. LIGHTNING effect on window shades up* L.C. MAN *appears from* L., *outside windows. His shadow shows on shades. He then disappears* R. *to terrace door. At same time* LIZZIE *appears at door* R. *with tray of dishes and food, Parker House roll, chop, plate, cup and saucer. She walks slowly, with her head turned to look behind her. The faint LIGHT of a candle from the hall off* R. *gives her enough light to advance. As she gets to* C., *above table, she hears key turn in terrace door. Registers fright. She has tray poised over the table.* MAN *who passed the windows now enters terrace door. He closes the door, reaches out his left arm, as if feeling his way to stairs. On his wrist he has a wrist watch with luminous face. It glows in*

darkness. LIZZIE *stands galvanized with fright.*
MAN *about to go up staircase.* LIZZIE *drops the*
tray on top of the table with a crash. She
makes three attempts to scream before her
voice responds. Then she shrieks. The MAN
quickly runs up the stairs and off R. CORNELIA
runs on R. *She is carrying a lighted candle. One*
candle LIGHTS come on and follow her to R.C.
CORNELIA *also carries a coffee pot, half filled*
with burnt sugar and water (coffee) and spills
it at every step. At same time DETECTIVE *enters*
L.3 *with candle lighted. ELECTRICIAN*
catch both these candle effects—one R., *one* L.
Follow lights to C. CORNELIA R.C. DETECTIVE
L.C. *Bring LIGHTS up center strips in foots*
and borders to two candle effect. With DETEC-
TIVE'S *candle and* CORNELIA'S *the room is now*
fairly illuminated.)

CORNELIA. For the love of Heaven, what's
wrong? (CORNELIA R. *of* LIZZIE. LIZZIE, *on drop-*
ping the tray, works around to front of table C. *and*
is looking up R.C. *when others enter.* CORNELIA,
holding the coffee pot inclined, the coffee pours out
of the spout on LIZZIE'S *foot.)*

LIZZIE. *(Screams)* Oh, my foot! My foot!

CORNELIA. *(*R.C.*)* My patience! Did you yell like
that because you stubbed your toe?

LIZZIE. *(Wildly)* You scalded it! It went up
the staircase.

CORNELIA. Your toe went up the staircase?

LIZZIE. *(Stands on one foot)* No, no! An eye—
as big as a saucer! It ran right up that staircase—
(CORNELIA *puts* C. *pot on table* C. *and candle on*
table.)

DETECTIVE. *(Sternly,* L.C. *down stage)* Now, see
here. Stop this chicken-on-one-leg business, and
tell me what you saw.

LIZZIE. *(Still holding up one leg)* A ghost! It came right through that door and went up the stairs! (DALE *and* BROOKS, *with lighted candle, come on from* R., *followed by* BILLY.)

DALE. Who screamed? *(Up* R.C. *above others.* BROOKS *stands above* R. *door.* BILLY *down* R. *below door* R.*)*

LIZZIE. I did. I saw a ghost. *(Then to* CORNELIA*)* I begged you not to come here. I begged you on my bended knees. There's a graveyard not a quarter of a mile away.

CORNELIA. *(*R.C.*)* Yes, and one more scare like that, Lizzie Allen, and you'll have me lying in it.

LIZZIE. *(Holding foot)* Oh, my foot! If anything tries to get me now, I won't even be able to run away. (BROOKS *up with candle.* CORNELIA *goes up to terrace door in alcove.)*

DETECTIVE. *(Sore)* Now, Lizzie—what did you really see?

LIZZIE. I told you what I saw.

DETECTIVE. *(Rather threateningly)* You're not trying to frighten Miss Van Gorder into leaving this house and going back to the city?

LIZZIE. *(Grimly)* Well, if I am, I'm giving myself a good scare too, ain't I?

CORNELIA. *(Coming down* R.C. *from terrace door; annoyed)* Somebody who had a key could have got in here, Mr. Anderson. That door's been unbolted from the inside.

LIZZIE. *(Hysterically)* I *told* you so! I *knew* something was going to happen tonight. I heard rappings all over the house today, and the Ouija Board spelled "Bat"!

DETECTIVE. *(Still* L.C.*)* I think I see the answer to your puzzle, Miss Van Gorder! An hysterical and not very reliable woman—(LIZZIE *glares at him)*—anxious to go back to the city, and terrified over and over by the shutting off of the electric light.

CORNELIA. I wonder!

DETECTIVE. A good night's sleep and——

LIZZIE. *(Interrupting, aghast)* My God! We're not going to bed, are we?

DETECTIVE. *(Kindly to* LIZZIE) You'll feel better in the morning. Lock your door and say your prayers and leave the rest to me.

CORNELIA. That's very good advice. You take her, Dale. (CORNELIA *puts arm around* LIZZIE. DALE *comes down* R. *of* CORNELIA. LIZZIE *is passed along by* CORNELIA *to* DALE, *who puts arm around her shoulder, leads her toward door* R.)

LIZZIE. *(Does not want to go, but does)* I'm not going to bed. Do you think I'm going to wake up in the morning with my throat cut? (DALE *and* LIZZIE *exit* R.)

DETECTIVE. *(Speaking to* CORNELIA) There are certain things I want to discuss with you, Miss Van Gorder, but they can wait till tomorrow morning.

CORNELIA. *(Looks off* R.) Do you think all this pure imagination?

DETECTIVE. *(Close to table* C.) Don't you?

CORNELIA. I'm not sure.

DETECTIVE. *(Laughs a little)* I'll tell you what I'll do. *(Puts candle down)* You go upstairs and go to bed comfortably. I'll make a careful search of the house before I settle down.

CORNELIA. *(Turns; looks at* DETECTIVE; *picks up coffee pot off table* C.) I'm afraid Lizzie has *absorbed* most of your coffee. Billy shall make you some more. *(She turns to* BILLY. *He steps forward and takes pot. Registers it is hot. He bows and exits with coffee pot* R.) Well, I hope we're at the end of our troubles. *(She crosses to table.* DETECTIVE *hands her candle.)*

DETECTIVE. Sure you are. Now you go upstairs.

(CORNELIA *has started* R. *with candle. ELECTRI-CIAN follow light to* R. DETECTIVE *goes up* L.C. *and then* R. *back of table*) Get your beauty sleep. I'm sure you need it. *(Earnestly, without intention, then realizing what he said.)*

CORNELIA. *(Has reached door* R., *turns, smiles caustically at him)* I begin to understand why The Bat has so long eluded you! *(Exits* R. *majestically.)*

DETECTIVE. *(Takes out handkerchief; mops his face)* Whew! *(Then looks at* BROOKS, *who stands above door* R. DETECTIVE *comes over* R.C.; *puts handkerchief away.* BROOKS *about to exit, when* DETECTIVE *speaks)* So you're the gardener, are you?

BROOKS. *(Lightly)* Yes.

DETECTIVE. Well, I don't need any gardening done just now—you can—— *(Looks attentively at* BROOKS; *step* R.) I've seen you somewhere—and I'll place you before long. *(There is a little threat in his voice)* Not in the portrait gallery at Headquarters, are you?

BROOKS. *(Resentfully)* Not yet.

DETECTIVE. Well, we slip up now and then. All right, Brooks. If you're needed during the night you'll be *called.*

BROOKS. Very well, sir. (BROOKS *exits* R. *Closes door.)*

(DETECTIVE *watches him off with expression of suspicion. With noiseless step,* DETECTIVE *goes to door* R.; *listens. Opens door suddenly. Then closes door. Takes out revolver. To table* C.; *picks up candle; goes up* R. *ELECTRICIAN follow candle, and DIM DOWN when* DETECTIVE *goes into alcove.* DETECTIVE *proceeds to make a careful search of the entry, floor, walls, stair and stair rail. He looks up staircase. Then bolts terrace door; comes back into room.*

ELECTRICIAN follow candle to table C. DE-
TECTIVE *draws revolver from hip pocket; examines it; then exits* R. *with candle. LIGHTS
OUT. WIND, THUNDER, LIGHTNING.
Pause.* DALE *comes down the stairs holding a
lighted candle high. She carries a rubber slick-
er and a pair of rubbers. She is cautious. She
unbolts the terrace door; comes into the room
from alcove. ELECTRICIAN catch her candle and follow to table* C. *This makes room
lighted with one candle. She places the candle
on table* C. *and sits* R. *of table; places coat on
back of chair. She is about to put on her rubbers when she hears a KNOCK on terrace door.
She starts at the sound, terrified, as she opens
drawer Right side of the table, takes out revolver. Steps up back of table* C. *with revolver
pointed up at alcove* R.C. FLEMING *makes
NOISE as if opening terrace door with key.)*

DICK. (DICK FLEMING *enters terrace door; closes
it. He steps into room from alcove; stands there a
moment. He is a man of perhaps thirty, rather dis-
sipated as to face, foppish in dress, with collar of his
dinner coat turned up against the rain. Up at door*
R.C.*)* Did I frighten you?

DALE. Oh, Mr. Fleming—yes! *(She puts revolver on table. She goes toward him.)*

DICK. I rapped—but as nobody heard me, I used
my key.

DALE. You're wet through.

DICK. Oh, no! *(Takes off cap and raincoat;
places them on back of chair* R.I*)* Reggie Beresford brought me over in his car. He's waiting down
the drive.

DALE. *(Goes up* R.C.*; closes double door; steps
down a few steps)* Mr. Fleming, I'm in dreadful
trouble!

DICK. *(Over a few steps to her)* I say! That's too bad.

DALE. You know the Union Bank closed today.

DICK. Yes, I know it! I didn't have anything in it—or in *any* bank, for that matter—but I hate to see the old thing go to smash.

DALE. Well, even if *you* haven't lost anything by this failure, a lot of your friends have, surely?

DICK. *(R.C.)* I'll say so! Beresford is sitting down the road in his Rolls-Royce now—writhing with pain!

DALE. *(Pause. Crosses above table to L.C.)* Lots of awfully poor people are going to suffer, too.

DICK. *(Rather heartlessly)* Oh, well, the poor are always in trouble. They specialize in suffering. *(Takes out cigarette case and cigarette; moves closer to table R.C.)* But look here—you didn't send for me to discuss the poor depositor, did you? Mind if I smoke?

DALE. No! (DICK *takes up candle from table; lights cigarette; slight pause.* DALE L.C. *across table)* Mr. Fleming, I'm going to say something rather brutal. Please don't mind. I'm merely desperate. You see, I happen to be engaged to the cashier— Jack Bailey.

DICK. *(Whistles and sits on edge of table)* I *see!* And he's beat it!

DALE. He has not! I'm going to tell you something—he's here now, in this house. My aunt thinks he's a new gardener. He is here, Mr. Fleming, because he knows he didn't take the money, and the only person who could have done it—was—your uncle. (DICK *drops cigarette on tray. Pause.* DICK *steps back, looks at* DALE, *then slowly crosses front of table to Left. Turns; faces her.)*

DICK. That's a pretty strong indictment to bring against a dead man.

DALE. It is true.

DICK. All right. *(Steps a little to* L. *Smiles)* Suppose it's true? Where do I come in? *(Steps toward her* R.; *faces her)* You don't think I know where the money is?

DALE. No, but I think you might help to find it. *(She turns, goes* R.C. *to make sure no one is listening, then back to* L.C.; *faces* FLEMING*)* If anybody comes in—you've just come to get something of yours. *(Comes close to him)* Do you know anything about a Hidden Room in this house?

DICK. A Hidden Room—that's good. *(Laughs)* Never heard of it. Now, let me get this straight. The idea is—a Hidden Room—and the money is in it—is that it?

DALE. *(Nods "yes")* The architect who built this house told Jack Bailey he had built a Hidden Room in it. *(*DICK's *expression has changed. A slowly growing look of avarice and calculation has taken the place of his smile. He no longer looks at* DALE. *His eyes are shifty and uncertain. They open and close as though already he has them on the treasure.)* Do you know where there are any blueprints of the house?

DICK. *(Starts; restrains himself)* Blueprints? *(It is evident to the audience that he does know.)* Why, there may be some—— *(He formulates; one can see almost the plot growing in his mind)* Have you looked in that old secretary in the morning room? My uncle used to keep all sorts of papers there.

DALE. Why, don't you remember, you locked it when we took the house?

DICK. *(Gets out his keyring and selects the key)* So I did. Suppose you go and look. Don't you think I'd better stay here? (DALE *takes key.)*

DALE. *(Cheerful; grateful)* Yes—— Oh, I can hardly thank you enough! *(She quickly crosses to* R. *and exits; closes door.)*

(DICK *quickly looks around room, then runs to
bookcase below door* R.; *then looks up* R.C.
Goes up to bookcase above door R., *then another
pause. Then to bookcase up* C. *Turns; looks
around room again. Pause. Decides to try the
other bookcase above fireplace and just below
door* L.3. *All these moves are quick. He takes
out the books in top shelf and puts them quickly on mantel at fireplace; reaches behind books
on shelf and pulls out a roll of three blueprints.
He leans over to see what they are at fireplace.
Then over to table* C.; *shoves back armchair* L.
of table C. *Holds blueprints close to candle on
table. Looking carefully at each blueprint, finds
the third one is the one he wants. He tears off
a corner of it.*)

DALE. (*Enters; closes door behind her* R. *Quickly
over to him, front of table,* C., *rejoiced*) Oh, you
found it! (*Gives him the key*) Please let me have
it. I *know* that's it.
DICK. (L.C. *His manner changed*) Just a moment. (*He steps away from her. Picking up candle
and looking at the piece of blueprint in his hand;
then turns; looks at* DALE) Do you suppose, if that
money is actually here, that I can simply turn this
over to you—and let you give it to Bailey? Every
man has his price. How do I know that Bailey's
isn't a million dollars? (*He inspects piece of blueprint closely.*)
DALE. What do you mean to do, then?
DICK. (*Turning over blueprint in his hand.
Pause*) I don't know. (*Puts candle down on table.
Looks at* DALE) What is it you want me to do?
DALE. Aren't you going to give it to me?
DICK. I'll have to think about that. So the missing cashier is in the house posing as a gardener?

DALE. If you won't give it to me—there's a detective in the house. *(She makes a turn to* R. *as if to call him. Then to* DICK*)* Give it to him—let him search.

DICK. *(Quickly, facing her, startled)* A detective? What's a detective doing here?

DALE. People have been trying to break in.

DICK. What people?

DALE. I don't know.

DICK. *(To himself, looking out front)* Then it *is* here. *(At this the* L. *door of the double doors up* R.C. *opens noiselessly just an inch or so. Evidently someone is listening.)* I'm not going to give it to the detective. *(*DICK *picks up the rolls of blueprints; quickly goes to fireplace over* L.2*; throws in the roll of blueprints.* ELECTRICIAN *works fire glow up and down.* DICK *takes the small piece of blueprint from pocket; watches papers burn.* DALE *has followed him over to fireplace.)*

DALE. *(As she follows* DICK *over* L.*)* What do you mean? What are you going to do?

DICK. *(Turns and faces* DALE, *near fireplace)* Let us suppose a few things, Miss Ogden. Suppose my price is a million dollars—suppose I need money very badly—and my uncle has left me a house containing that amount in cash—suppose I choose to consider that that money is mine—then it wouldn't be hard to suppose, would it, that I'd make a pretty sincere attempt to get it?

DALE. *(Close up to him)* If you go out of this room with that paper, I'll scream for help.

DICK. To carry on our little game of supposing—suppose there is a detective in this house—and that if I were cornered I should tell him where to lay his hands on Jack Bailey, do you suppose you would scream? *(*DALE *stands helpless. He quickly crosses her, front of table* C.*; stops* R. *of table, looks up at*

R.C. *doors a moment, then he hurries up and opens them; makes for stairs in alcove.)*

DALE. *(Follows him over to table* C. *When he starts for* R.C. *she picks up revolver off table and hurries up after him. Speaks as she goes. Suddenly desperate)* No! No! Give it to me! Give it to me! *(*DALE *up to* DICK *at foot of stairs in alcove. He turns and waits for her. He snatches the revolver from her. A very short scuffle in the darkness of the entry in effort to secure the revolver. He unguards the piece of blueprint, which she tears from him, leaving only a corner of it in his grasp.)*

(A SPOT LIGHT flashes on from the top of stairs off R. *and covers* DICK *at foot of stairs. Supposed to be a pocket flash, held by an invisible hand. Light shows him poised ready to come down after the girl, his face shown distorted with fury. SHOT off stage. As* DICK *falls to floor, LIGHT OFF.* DICK *falls forward, dead. The revolver* DALE *carried falls between them.* DICK *lies with head just inside the double doors into the room proper, face downward.)*

DALE. *(Backs away into room* L. *and above table; hides the blueprint in dress. With a little whimpering cry of horror)* Oh, no, no! *(The STORM dies out. Pause. Count fifteen; then VOICES off* R. *heard ad lib.)*

VOICES. The noise came from this room—I think it is in here.

(LIGHTS flash on full up—Foots—Border—Lamps and Brackets. Count five. General Entrance. (1) DETECTIVE. *He goes well on; sees body up* R.C. *(2)* BROOKS. *He goes up* R.C. *beyond doors. (3)* BILLY, *the Jap. Stands above door* R. *(4)*

CORNELIA. *Comes in, and down* R. *below door* R. LIZZIE *enters last and stands in doorway* R. NOTE: CORNELIA *has commenced undressing and is in a dressing-gown and* LIZZIE *is in old flannelette wrapper. They all perceive* DALE *and the body. A tense silence.)*

DALE. *(Stepping back until she is almost to door* L.3*)* Oh! I didn't do it! I didn't do it!

                      (WARN Curtain.)

DETECTIVE. *(Goes to body* R.C.; *examines it; takes plenty of time)* He's dead. *(Pause. Picks up revolver, looks at it, then turns and goes to* C., *above table; looks at* DALE *curiously)* Who is he?

DALE. *(Hysterically)* Richard Fleming— Somebody shot him!

DETECTIVE. *(Takes a step toward her)* What do you mean by somebody? (CORNELIA *sinks into chair down* R.I.)

DALE. Oh, I don't know. *(Hysterically)* Somebody on the staircase.

DETECTIVE. Did you see anybody?

DALE. No—there was a light from somewhere— like a pocket flash.

LIZZIE. *(In doorway* R.; *hysterically points up at stairs)* I *told* you I saw a man go up that staircase. *(Pause.* DETECTIVE *has turned from facing* DALE. *He looks at* LIZZIE *and* CORNELIA *over* R.)*

CORNELIA. *(Down* R.I*)* That's the only explanation, Mr. Anderson.

DETECTIVE. I've been all over the house. There's nobody there. *(HOUSE PHONE rings. Above door* R.)*

CORNELIA. *(Rises. Slight pause.* CORNELIA *takes one step up* R., *then turns)* The house phone—— *(Looks at the other characters)* But we're all here.

(They ALL *stand, pause, aghast. Then* CORNELIA *goes up to phone)* Hello! Hello! (ALL *stand, listening rigidly. She gasps. An expression of horror comes over her face.)*

THE CURTAIN SLOWLY FALLS

ACT TWO

DISCO'ERED: ALL CHARACTERS *as at end of Act I. The action being continuous. They are staring aghast at* CORNELIA, *who still stands clutching the phone.*
Only exception. LIZZIE *seated down* R.1, *face up stage.*

CORNELIA. *(Gasps)* Somebody groaning! It's horrible! (DETECTIVE *crosses to* CORNELIA. *She gives him the phone. She steps down* R.C. *to table.)*

DETECTIVE. *(Listens in phone)* I don't hear anything. *(Slight pause.)*

CORNELIA. I heard it! I couldn't *imagine* such a dreadful sound! I tell you somebody in this house is in terrible distress.

DETECTIVE. Where does this phone connect?

CORNELIA. Practically every room in the house.

DETECTIVE. *(Puts receiver to ear again)* Just what did you hear?

CORNELIA. Dreadful groans, and what seemed to be an inarticulate effort to speak.

LIZZIE. *(Trembling violently)* I'd go somewhere, if I had somewhere to go! *(Rises.)*

CORNELIA. *(Faces up to* DETECTIVE) Won't you send these men to investigate? Or go yourself?

DETECTIVE. My place is here—you two men. *(To* BROOKS *and* BILLY) Take another look through the house. (BILLY *opens door* R.) Don't leave the building—I'll want you pretty soon.

51

BROOKS. If you'll give me that revolver—— *(Indicating* CORNELIA'S *revolver, which* DETECTIVE *still holds in his hand.)*

DETECTIVE. This revolver will stay where it is. *(Exit* BILLY, *followed by* BROOKS, R. *Close door. As* BROOKS *goes reluctantly, puzzled and anxious glance at* DALE, DETECTIVE *goes step* R., *looks at body, then turns quickly on* DALE*)* Now I want the real story. You lied before.

CORNELIA. *(Down* L.C.; *indignantly)* That is no tone to use! You'll only terrify her.

DETECTIVE. *(Turns; looks at* CORNELIA*)* Where were you when this happened? *(*DALE *moves down* L. *a little.)*

CORNELIA. Upstairs in my room.

DETECTIVE. *(To* LIZZIE*)* And you?

LIZZIE. In *my* room, brushing Miss Cornelia's hair.

DETECTIVE. *(*R.C. *to table; breaks revolver and looks at it)* One shot has been fired from this revolver.

CORNELIA. *(Looking over shoulder)* I fired it myself, this afternoon.

DETECTIVE. *(Comes down* R.C.*)* You're a quick thinker. *(Places revolver on table* C.*)*

CORNELIA. I demand that you get the Coroner here.

LIZZIE. Doctor Wells is the Coroner.

DETECTIVE. *(*R.C. *to* DALE*)* I'm going to ask you some questions.

CORNELIA. Do you mind covering that body first? *(*DETECTIVE *eyes her in a rather ugly fashion, then gets* FLEMING'S *raincoat on chair down* R. *Goes up to body. Throws coat over it.)* Shall I telephone for the Coroner?

DETECTIVE. *(Goes up* C. *to phone)* I'll do it. What's his number?

DALE. *(L.)* He's not at his office—he's at the Johnsons'.

CORNELIA. *(Up to phone C.)* I'll get the Johnsons, Mr. Anderson. *(DETECTIVE relinquishes phone to CORNELIA; gives her a look; crosses over to L.C. upstage.)*

DETECTIVE. *(To DALE)* Now what was Fleming doing here? *(DALE down to chair L. at fireplace.)*

DALE. I don't know.

DETECTIVE. Well, I'll ask that question another way. How did he get into the house?

CORNELIA. *(At phone up C.)* One—four——

DALE. He had a key. He used to live here.

DETECTIVE. A key to what door?

DALE. To that door over there. *(Indicating terrace door.)*

CORNELIA. *(At phone)* Hello—is that Mr. Johnson's residence? Is Doctor Wells there? No? *(DETECTIVE turns during this; watches CORNELIA. CORNELIA pauses; listens in on phone)* All right, thank you. Good night! *(Hangs up phone, puzzled. She comes down to R.C. at table C. Same time DETECTIVE registers, sees ashes of blueprints in fireplace.)*

DETECTIVE. *(Steps back to L.C. To DALE)* When did you take that revolver out of the table drawer?

DALE. When I heard him outside, on the terrace, I was frightened.

LIZZIE. *(Tiptoes over to CORNELIA, R.C.)* You wanted a detective! I hope you're happy now you've got one! *(CORNELIA gives LIZZIE a look. LIZZIE goes back to R.I.)*

DETECTIVE. *(To DALE)* When he came in, what did he say to you? *(CORNELIA sits R. of table.)*

DALE. Just—something about the weather.

DETECTIVE. You didn't have any quarrel with him?

DALE. *(After hesitation)* No.

DETECTIVE. He just came in that door—said something about the weather—and was shot from that staircase? Is that it?

DALE. *(After moment's hesitation)* Yes.

CORNELIA. *(*R.C. *at table)* Are all these questions necessary? You can't for a moment believe that Miss Ogden shot that man? (DALE *sits at fireplace.)*

DETECTIVE. *(Looks at* DALE*)* I think she knows more than she's telling. She's concealing something. The nephew of the President of the Union Bank shot in his own house on the day the Bank has failed—that's queer enough. *(He turns; looks at* CORNELIA*)* But when the only person present at his murder is the girl who is engaged to the guilty cashier—— *(Looks at* DALE*)* I want to know more about it! *(Picks up cigarette* DICK *put on ash tray Act I.)*

CORNELIA. *(Rises)* Is that true, Dale?

DALE. Yes.

CORNELIA. What has *that* got to do with it? *(To* DETECTIVE.*)*

DETECTIVE. *(Turning to* CORNELIA*)* I'm not accusing this girl, but behind every crime there is a motive. When we've found the motive for *this* crime we'll have found the criminal.

(ELECTRICIAN ready to work Bat Light, L. *to* R., *across windows up* L.C. DALE'S *hand instinctively goes to her bosom where she has concealed the blueprint. Her expression shows that she realizes that her having the blueprint is damaging evidence against her.)*

DETECTIVE. *(Who has been facing* CORNELIA, *now turns on* DALE*)* What papers did he burn in that grate? *(Slight pause.)*

DALE. Papers!

DETECTIVE. Papers! The ashes are still there.

CORNELIA. Miss Ogden has said he didn't come into this room.

DETECTIVE. I hold in my hand proof that he was in this room for some time. *(Holding up half-burnt cigarette.* CORNELIA *sits.)* His cigarette with his monogram on it. *(He goes to fireplace, above* DALE, *and picks up small piece of blueprint from the fender. Back to* L.C.; *looks at* DALE*)* A fragment of what is technically known as a blueprint. What were you and Richard Fleming doing with a blueprint? (DALE *hesitates.)* Now think it over! The truth will come out sooner or later! Better be frank *now!*

BROOKS. *(Runs on* R., *followed by* BILLY. *Up to* R.C. BILLY R. *above door.* BROOKS, *a trifle breathlessly)* Nothing in the house, sir.

BILLY. Me go all over house. Nobody. (BOTH *start for* R. *as if to continue search.)*

DETECTIVE. You men stay here! I want to ask you some questions. *(Then to* DALE*)* Now, what about this blueprint?

DALE. *(Still seated)* I'll tell you just what happened. I sent for Richard Fleming, and when he came I asked him if he knew where there were any blueprints of the house.

DETECTIVE. *Why* did you want blueprints?

DALE. Because I believed old Mr. Fleming took the money himself, from the Union Bank, and *hid* it here.

DETECTIVE. Where did you get that idea?

DALE. I won't tell you.

DETECTIVE. What had the blueprints to do with it?

DALE. I'd heard there was a Hidden Room built in the house.

DETECTIVE. *(Leans forward)* Did you locate that room?

DALE. *(Hesitates)* No.

DETECTIVE. Then why did you burn the blue-prints?

DALE. *He* burned them. I don't *know* why.

DETECTIVE. Then you didn't locate this Hidden Room?

DALE. No.

DETECTIVE. Did he?

CORNELIA. What's that? (DALE *rises.*)

DETECTIVE. What's what?

CORNELIA. I heard something.

(THEY ALL *turn and look up stage at windows* L.C. BROOKS *up* C. *near windows.* BILLY R. *of him.* CORNELIA R.C. *at table.* DETECTIVE *over* L. DALE *down* L. *Suddenly from outside a circle of brilliant white LIGHT is thrown on the window shades up stage. In the* C. *of the light area is seen a vivid black shadow resembling a gigantic Black Bat. For an instant it glows there, travelling from* L. *to* R., *and disappears.*)

LIZZIE. *(Over* R.I; *wails)* Oh, my God—it's The Bat! That's his sign. (BROOKS *starts for terrace door.*)

CORNELIA. Wait, Brooks! *(Then to* DETECTIVE*)* Mr. Anderson, you are familiar with the sign of The Bat. Did that look like it?

DETECTIVE. *(Puzzled and evidently disturbed)* Well—it looked like the shadow of a bat—I'll say that. *(DOORBELL rings.* ALL *look at door* R.)

BROOKS. I'll answer that!

CORNELIA. *(Gives him key off table* C.) Don't admit anyone till you know who it is.

(BROOKS *exits* R. ALL *stand and wait.* CORNELIA, *hand over her revolver on table where* DETEC-TIVE *had laid it.* BROOKS *and* WELLS' *voices heard off* R., *raised in angry dispute. Some evidence of a slight scuffle. Ad lib. "What do I know about a flashlight?" "I haven't got a pocket flash." "Take your hands off me." Then* WELLS *enters* R., *cap on, followed by* BROOKS. *He comes down* R.; *faces* CORNELIA, *who is* R.C. *He is ruffled and enraged.* BROOKS *close behind him, and then to* L. *of him, vigilant and watchful.* CORNELIA, *relieved, quickly drops revolver.)*

DOCTOR. My dear Miss Van Gorder! Won't you instruct your servants that, even if I do make a late call, I am not to be received with violence. *(Takes off cap; bag on chair* R. *of table* C.*)*

BROOKS. *(Strong)* I asked you if you had a pocket flash about you. If you call a question like that violence——

CORNELIA. It's all right, Brooks. (BROOKS *places key on table and goes up* R.C.*)* You see, Dr. Wells, just a moment before you rang the doorbell a circle of white light was thrown on those window shades.

DOCTOR. *(Down* R.*)* Why—that was probably the searchlight from my car—I noticed as I drove up that it fell directly on that window.

LIZZIE. *(With deep suspicion)* "He may be a merchant, a lawyer, a doctor——"

CORNELIA. *(Suspiciously watching the* DOCTOR. *Lift scene)* In the center of this ring of light there was an almost perfect silhouette of a bat.

DOCTOR. A bat? Ah—I see—the symbol of the criminal of that name. *(Laughs)* I think I can explain what you saw—quite often my lamps collect insects at night. A large moth spread on the glass would give precisely the effect you speak of. Just to satisfy you—I'll go out and take a look. *(He turns and is about to go up* R.C. *when he sees body on floor. At same time* CORNELIA, *to front of table* L.C., *turns and faces up to* DOCTOR.*) Why—— (Startled, stares at covered body. Then he glances from covered body on floor to the faces of the* OTHERS.*)*

CORNELIA. *(*L.C. *at table, facing* DOCTOR, *who is up* R.C.*)* We have had a very sad occurrence here, Doctor.

DOCTOR. *(Turns; looks at* CORNELIA*)* Who?

CORNELIA. Richard Fleming.

DOCTOR. *(Pause. Horrified)* Richard Fleming! *(Bends over body; turns raincoat back.)*

CORNELIA. Shot and killed, from that staircase.

DETECTIVE. *(Up* L.C.*)* Shot and killed, anyhow.

DOCTOR. *(On knees,* R. *of body. He has been blithe and gay up to that moment; seems almost instantly to become aged. His face is stricken. He repeats)* From that stairway. *(Rises. Straightens up and glances up the stairs, then)* What was Richard Fleming doing in this house at this hour?

DETECTIVE. That's what I'm trying to find out. *(*DOCTOR *looks over at* DETECTIVE. DOCTOR *is puzzled.)*

CORNELIA. Doctor—this is Mr. Anderson. *(*DOCTOR *crosses to* DETECTIVE L.C. *above table. They shake hands.)*

DETECTIVE. *(To* DOCTOR*)* Headquarters!

LIZZIE. *(Crosses from* R.I *to table* R.C. *Loud whisper to* CORNELIA*)* Don't you let him fool you with any of that moth business. He's The Bat! *(She sits* R. *of table* C.*)*

CORNELIA. *(To* DOCTOR*)* I didn't tell you, Doctor, I sent for a detective this afternoon. *(Then suspiciously)* You happened in very opportunely.

DOCTOR. *(Pulling himself together)* After I left the Johnsons I felt very uneasy. I determined to make one more effort to get you away from this house. As this shows, my fears were *justified.* *(*CORNELIA *sits* L.C. DOCTOR *takes off muffler; puts it in pocket of overcoat. Takes off overcoat; throws*

*it upstage on settee, front of French windows. He
takes out handkerchief, mops face and neck as
though under great mental excitement. Looks over
at body, then looks at* CORNELIA) Died instantly, I
suppose. *(Looks* L. *at* DETECTIVE*)* Didn't have time
to say anything?

DETECTIVE. *(Looking at* DALE*)* Ask the young
lady. She was here when it happened. (DOCTOR
looks at DALE.*)*

DALE. *(Pitifully)* He just fell over.

DOCTOR. *(There is no question but that the* DOC-
TOR *is relieved. He draws a long breath. Looking
at body. Speaks as he moves to* R.C. *Crosses above
table)* Poor Dick has proved my case for me better
than I expected. *(Stops* R.C. *Turns; looks at* DE-
TECTIVE, *who stands up* L.*)* Mr. Anderson, I ask
you to use your influence to see that these two ladies
find some safer spot than this for the night.

LIZZIE. *(Half rises)* Two? If you *know* any
safe spot, lead *me* to it! (DOCTOR *up to body.)*

CORNELIA. *(To* L. *of table* C.*)* I have a strange
feeling that I'm being watched by unfriendly eyes.

(BILLY *up to window, scared, pulls shade aside,
looks out; sees something outside when he looks
out window. Moves down while the others are
not looking at him. Pretending to straighten the
tray which* LIZZIE *brought on in Act I, he gets
possession of front door key, table* C., *and exits*
R. LIZZIE *speaks on word cue; does not wait for*
BILLY'S *business.)*

LIZZIE. *(Clutching at* CORNELIA, *across table)* I
wish the lights would go out again. (CORNELIA *slaps*
LIZZIE.*)* No, I don't neither! (LIZZIE *crosses to
door* R.; *stands there.)*

DETECTIVE. *(Steps to* C., *above table. To* DOC-

TOR*)* You say, Doctor, you came back to take these women away from the house. Why?

DOCTOR. *(Up* R.C., *back of chair)* Miss Van Gorder has explained.

CORNELIA. *(*L.C. *at table. To* DOCTOR*)* Mr. Anderson has already formed a theory of the crime.

DETECTIVE. *(Up* L.*)* I haven't said that. *(HOUSE PHONE up* R. *rings.* ALL *are startled. Turn; look at phone.* CORNELIA *and* DALE *rise.)*

DALE. *(Down* L.*)* The house telephone—again! *(*CORNELIA *makes movement as if to answer it.)*

DETECTIVE. *(Going to phone across above table. Takes up phone* R.*)* I'll answer that! Hello! Hello! *(The* DOCTOR'S *face is a study in fear. He clutches the back of chair* R. *of table* C. *to steady himself)* There's nobody there! *(Hangs up phone)* Where's that Jap? *(Looking at door* R. DALE, *relieved, sits down* L. LIZZIE *sits* R.I.*)*

CORNELIA. He just went out.

DETECTIVE. *(*R. *of* DOCTOR, *to* DOCTOR*)* That Jap rang that phone. Miss Van Gorder believes that this murder is the culmination of the series of mysterious happenings which caused her to send for me. I do not.

CORNELIA. Then what is the significance of the anonymous letters? Of the man Lizzie saw going up the stairs, of the attempt to break into the house? Of the ringing of that telephone bell?

DETECTIVE. *(Deliberately)* Terrorization.

DOCTOR. *(Moistening his dry lips)* By whom?

DETECTIVE. *(With cold deliberation)* I imagine by Miss Van Gorder's own servants. By that woman. *(Points at* LIZZIE. LIZZIE *rises.)* Who probably writes the letters—by the gardener, who may have been the man Lizzie saw slipping up the stairs—by the Jap, who goes out and rings the telephone.

CORNELIA. With what object?

DETECTIVE. That's what I'm going to find out.

CORNELIA. Absurd—the butler was in this room when the telephone rang the first time.

(Ad lib. NOISE between BERESFORD and BILLY off R. Violent scuffle. ALL turn at door R. Door opens and REGINALD BERESFORD is catapulted into the room by BILLY. BERESFORD falls to floor well down R.C. BILLY stands in doorway, arms folded; he is impassive. BERESFORD speaks as he picks himself up; brushes clothes off. He is in dinner clothes; carries straw hat.)

BERESFORD. *(Turning on BILLY)* Damn you! What do you mean by this?

BILLY. *(Impassively, in doorway R.)* Jui Jitsu. Pretty good stuff. Found on terrace with searchlight.

DETECTIVE. With searchlight!

BERESFORD. Well, why shouldn't I be on the terrace with a searchlight? *(CORNELIA crosses front of table to R. side of table C.)*

DETECTIVE. *(Steps down L. of BERESFORD)* Who are you?

BERESFORD. *(R.C.)* Who are you? *(DETECTIVE flashes his police badge, which is on inside of lapel of coat, right side. BERESFORD looks at it)* H'm! *(Takes out gold cigarette case)* Very pretty—nice, neat design—very chaste! *(He takes a swift glance around room; sees DALE over L.; suddenly senses the situation without suspecting a tragedy.)*

DETECTIVE. If you've finished admiring my badge, I'd like to know what you were doing on that terrace? .

BERESFORD. *(Hesitates, glances at DALE, then)* I've had some trouble with my car down the road.

(Looks again at DALE*)* I came to ask if I might telephone.

CORNELIA. Did it require a searchlight to find the house?

BERESFORD. Look here—why are you asking me all these questions?

CORNELIA. *(Stepping* R. *toward* BERESFORD*)* Do you mind letting me see that flashlight? (DETECTIVE *crosses up* C. BERESFORD *hands it to her. She examines it.* DETECTIVE *takes it from her; examines lens, then down* R. *of* BERESFORD. CORNELIA *gives way for* DETECTIVE. *She is now* R.C. *at table.)*

DETECTIVE. *(To* BERESFORD*)* Now—what's your name? *(Hands flash back to* BERESFORD.*)*

BERESFORD. *(Sulkily)* Beresford—Reginald Beresford—if you doubt it—I've probably got a card somewhere. *(Goes through his pockets.)*

DETECTIVE. What's your business?

BERESFORD. What's my business *here?*

DETECTIVE. *(Sharply)* How do you earn your living?

BERESFORD. *(Flippantly)* I don't. I'm a *lawyer.*

LIZZIE. *(Sepulchrally, quoting from newspaper)* "He may be a lawyer."

DETECTIVE. *(To* BERESFORD*)* And you came here to telephone about your car?

DALE. Oh, don't you see—he's trying to protect me—— It's no use, Mr. Beresford. (CORNELIA *turns, and steps* L. *beyond chair* L. *of table.* DALE *comes over to* L. *of table.* CORNELIA *places* DALE *in chair* L. *of table, placing her hand on* DALE'S *shoulder.)*

BERESFORD. *(*R.*)* I see. Well, the plain truth is—I didn't know the situation—and I thought I'd play safe, for Miss Ogden's sake.

DALE. *(To* DETECTIVE*)* He doesn't know anything about—*(Pause)*—this. He brought Mr. Fleming here in his car—that's all.

DETECTIVE. *(To* BERESFORD*)* Is that true?

BERESFORD. Yes—I got tired waiting and so I—

DETECTIVE. *(Breaks in curtly)* All right——
(Turns; takes a step up R.C.*)* Now, Doctor. *(Nods toward body.* BERESFORD *turns, follows* DETECTIVE'S *glance, stands rigid.)*

BERESFORD. *(Tensely)* What's that? *(*DOCTOR *uncovers body and kneels beside it.* BERESFORD, *thickly)* That's nct—Fleming—is it? *(Looks at* DETECTIVE, *who is up* R.C. DETECTIVE *nods head.)*

DOCTOR. If you've looked over the ground— *(To* DETECTIVE*)* I'll move the body to where I can have a better light.

BERESFORD. *(Takes another step up and says, with force)* Do you mean to say that Dick Fleming—— *(*DOCTOR *takes paper from* DICK'S *hand; throws cigarette to floor as he starts up.)*

DETECTIVE. *(Interrupting, eyes on* DOCTOR, *silences* BERESFORD *with an uplifted hand. Then, menacingly, to* DOCTOR*)* What have you got there, Doctor?

DOCTOR. *(On knees beside body)* What do you mean?

DETECTIVE. You took something just then, out of Fleming's hand.

DOCTOR. I took nothing out of his hand.

DETECTIVE. I warn you not to obstruct the course of Justice. Give it here.

DOCTOR. *(Gets up, and hands* DETECTIVE *small piece of blueprint he took out of* FLEMING'S *hand)* Why, it's a scrap of paper—— Nothing at all. *(*DOCTOR *crosses around body to* R. *side.)*

DETECTIVE. *(With blueprint, down to back of table* C., *eyes the* DOCTOR*)* Scraps of paper are sometimes very important. *(Looks at* DALE.*)*

BERESFORD. *(Angry. Crosses few steps over and up to* DETECTIVE, R.C.*)* Look here—I've got a right to know about this thing. I brought Fleming over here—and I want to know what happened to him.

LIZZIE. *(Down R.I, overcome)* You don't have to be a mind-reader to know that!

BERESFORD. *(To* DETECTIVE*)* Who killed him? That's what *I* want to know.

DETECTIVE. Well, you're not alone in that.

DOCTOR. *(Nervously)* As the Coroner—if Mr. Anderson is satisfied—I suggest that the body be taken where I can make a thorough examination. (DETECTIVE *up to body; turns body half over, then lets it fall back on face. Same as before.* DETECTIVE *steps back; glances from blueprint in his hand to* DOCTOR. DETECTIVE *takes off the overcoat from body; drops it up* R.C.*)*

DETECTIVE. All right. *(Comes down little* R.C.*)*

CORNELIA. Into the library, please. (CORNELIA *goes over to fireplace while body is being moved.* DALE *watches* DETECTIVE. DOCTOR, *in alcove, takes hold of body by legs.* BERESFORD, *right side, hands* BILLY *his hat, takes body under arm.* BROOKS, *left side, under arm.* DOCTOR *going off first below stairs and* R. BILLY *comes up* R. DETECTIVE, L. *of* BILLY, *also comes up.* DETECTIVE *follows body off. As body disappears,* LIZZIE *up to double doors. Then* BILLY *picks up the rug, up* R.C., *where* DETECTIVE *dropped it.* BILLY *exits* R. *with rug.* DALE *gets piece of blueprint from front of dress and gets roll from floor, front of table,* C. *She puts blueprint in the roll, replaces roll on floor.* BILLY *returns from* R. *door. Enters; goes to table; picks up tray. Sees roll on floor; places it on tray; turns with tray; takes a step* R. DETECTIVE *comes back on as* BILLY *enters* R.*)*

CORNELIA. Take that tray out to the dining room.

DETECTIVE. *(Steps down in front of him,* R.C.*)* Wait, I'll look at that tray. *(Makes a thorough search of the tray; even examines the napkin, lifts* *the dishes, etc.* DALE *sits, tensely apprehensive.* DETECTIVE *fails to find anything)* All right, take it away. (BILLY *exits* R. *with tray.)*

CORNELIA. *(Crosses to* R.C.*)* Lizzie, go out in the kitchen and make some fresh coffee. I'm sure we'll all need it.

LIZZIE. Go out in that kitchen—alone.

CORNELIA. *(Sits* R.C.*)* Billy's there.

LIZZIE. That Jap and his jui jitsu! One twist, and I'd be folded up like a pretzel! *(Exits* R.*)*

DETECTIVE. *(To back of table* C. *Looks at piece of blueprint in his hand, and then at* DALE*)* Now, Miss Ogden—I have here a scrap of blueprint which was in Dick Fleming's hand when he was killed. I'll trouble you for the rest of it.

DALE. *(Is seated* L. *of table* C.*)* The rest of it?

DETECTIVE. Don't tell me that he started to go out of this house holding a blank scrap of blue paper in his hand. He didn't start to go out at all!

DALE. *(Rises and goes* L. *one step)* Why do you say that?

DETECTIVE. His cap's there on that table.

CORNELIA. *(Is seated* R.C. *of table* C. *Disturbed)* If you're keeping anything back, Dale, tell him.

DETECTIVE. *(Crosses down* L.C.*)* She's keeping something back, all right. She's told part of the truth but not all. You and Fleming located that room by means of a blueprint of the house. He started—not to go out, but probably to go up that staircase. And he had in his hand the rest of this. *(He holds out the scrap of blueprint.)*

DALE. *(Slight pause, then, rather pitifully)* He was going to take the money and go away with it.

CORNELIA. *(Alarmed)* Dale!

DALE. He changed the minute he heard about it. He was all kindness before that, but afterwards—— *(She closes her eyes; crosses to* L.*)*

DETECTIVE. *(Turns triumphantly to* CORNELIA*)*

She started in to find the money—and save Bailey, but to do it she had to take Fleming into her confidence, and he turned yellow. Rather than let him get away with it—she—— *(He makes expressive gesture, hand on hip pocket.* DALE *registers. He indicates revolver. Then to* DALE*)* Is that true?

DALE. *(Step down* L.*)* I didn't kill him.

DETECTIVE. Why didn't you call for help? You—you knew I was here?

DALE. *(Hesitates)* I couldn't. *(Step toward him, then step back* L.*)*

CORNELIA. *(Agitated)* Dale! Be careful what you say!

DETECTIVE. *(Advances step to* DALE*)* Now I mean to find out two things—*why* you didn't call for help, and *what* you have done with the blueprint.

DALE. Suppose I could find that piece of blueprint for you? Would that establish Jack Bailey's innocence?

DETECTIVE. If the money's there—yes.

CORNELIA. *(Rises, crosses to* L. *and to* DALE; *turns on* DETECTIVE*)* But her own guilt! No, Mr. Anderson—granting that she knows where that paper is—and she has not said that she does, I shall want more time, and much legal advice, before I allow her to turn it over to you.

(Enter from below the stairs, DOCTOR, BERESFORD *and* BROOKS *silently.* BROOKS *stands well up* R.C.*)*

DETECTIVE. *(Turns and looks up at them)* Well, Doctor?

DOCTOR. *(Up* R.C.*)* Well, poor fellow—straight through the heart!

CORNELIA. *(Over* L.*)* Were there any powder marks?

DOCTOR. No—and the clothing was not burned. He was apparently shot from some little distance—and I should say, from above. *(Comes down R.I.)*

DETECTIVE. Beresford, did Fleming tell you why he came here tonight? (BERESFORD *crosses over and up to* R.C. DETECTIVE *over to back of table* C.)

BERESFORD. No. He seemed to be in a great hurry; said Miss Ogden had telephoned for him, and asked me to drive him over.

DETECTIVE. Why did you come up to the house?

BERESFORD. Well—— *(Looks over at* DALE, *who is* L.) I thought it was putting rather a premium on friendship to keep me sitting out in the rain all night, so I came up the drive, and by the way—— *(Suddenly remembering)* I picked this up, about a hundred feet from the house. *(Pulls out a man's battered open-face silver watch from pocket; holds it out on his hand)* A man's watch. It was partly crushed into the ground, and you see it's stopped running.

DETECTIVE. *(Taking it, and examining it)* Yes! *(Thoughtfully)* At ten-thirty——

BERESFORD. I was using my pocket flash to find my way, and what first attracted my attention was the ground torn up. Anyone here recognize the watch? (DETECTIVE *shows watch, holding it up so* ALL *can see it. No one replies.)* You didn't hear any evidence of a struggle, did you?

CORNELIA. Just about ten-thirty Lizzie heard somebody cry out, in the grounds. (DETECTIVE *looks* BERESFORD *over.)*

BERESFORD. I don't suppose it has any bearing on this case, but it's interesting. (DETECTIVE, *having finished his examination of the watch, slips it into his pocket.)*

CORNELIA. *(Suspiciously)* Do you always carry a flashlight, Mr. Beresford?

BERESFORD. Always at night in the car.

DETECTIVE. This is all you found?

BERESFORD. Yes.

CORNELIA. *(Sits L. of table C.)* Some day I hope to meet the real estate agent who promised me that I would sleep here as I never slept before. He's right. I've slept with my clothes on every night since I came.

BILLY. *(Enters hurriedly R. He carries a butcher knife in one hand, his face is excited; comes on to R.C. To CORNELIA)* Key, kitchen door, please.

CORNELIA. Key? What for?

BILLY. Somebody outside try to get in. I see knob turn so—— *(Illustrating turning hand)* And so—three times. *(They are all startled.)*

DETECTIVE. *(Quickly puts hand to revolver in pocket)* You're sure of that, are you? *(Roughly to BILLY.)*

BILLY. Sure I sure!

DETECTIVE. *(Looks at CORNELIA, who is L.C.)* Where's that hysterical woman, Lizzie? She may get a bullet in her if she's not careful. *(DALE sits fireplace.)*

BILLY. She see too. She shut in closet. Say prayers maybe.

DETECTIVE. Doctor, have you a revolver?

DOCTOR. No.

DETECTIVE. How about you, Beresford?

BERESFORD. *(Hesitates)* Yes. Always carry one at night in the country. *(CORNELIA registers this.)*

DETECTIVE. Beresford, will you go with this Jap to the kitchen? *(Exit BILLY R., leaving door open.)* If anyone's working at the knob, shoot through the door. I'm going round to take a look outside. *(Starts up for doors R.C.)*

BERESFORD. *(Going to door R., turns, looks up at DETECTIVE. DETECTIVE stops, looks at BERESFORD as he speaks)* I advise you not to turn the doorknob yourself, then.

DETECTIVE. Much obliged. *(Exit* DETECTIVE *terrace door. Closes door. At same time* BERESFORD *exits* R.*)*

BROOKS. *(To* BERESFORD*)* I'll go with you if you don't mind. *(Exit* BROOKS R., *closing door.* DOCTOR *crosses up to below staircase.)*

CORNELIA. *(*L.C. *at table, to* DOCTOR*)* Doctor.

DOCTOR. Yes?

CORNELIA. Have *you* any theory about this occurrence tonight? *(Watching him closely.)*

DOCTOR. *(Down* R.*)* None whatever—it's beyond me.

CORNELIA. And yet you warned me to leave the house. *(Stop knitting)* You didn't have any reason to believe that the situation was even as serious as it has proved to be?

DOCTOR. I did the perfectly obvious thing when I warned you. Those letters made a distinct threat.

CORNELIA. *(Pause)* You said he'd probably been shot from above.

DOCTOR. Yes, apparently.

CORNELIA. *(Suddenly)* Have you a pocket flash, Doctor?

DOCTOR. *(Hesitates)* Why—yes—a flashlight is more important to a country doctor than castor oil.

CORNELIA. *(Turns to* DALE, *who is over* L.*)* Dale, you said you saw a white light shining down from above?

DALE. Yes.

CORNELIA. *(Crosses front of table* C. *to* DOCTOR *over* R.C.*)* May I borrow your flashlight? (DOCTOR *gives her his pocket flash.)* Now that I've got that fool detective out of the way, I want to do something. *(Crosses to* R.*)* Doctor, I shall ask you to stand at the foot of the small staircase, facing up.

DOCTOR. Now?

CORNELIA. Now, please. (DOCTOR *walks up into alcove, takes position foot of stairs.* CORNELIA *crosses to* R., *turns, looks at* DALE*)* And, Dale—when I give the word, put out the lights here, and then tell me when I have reached the point on the staircase from which the flashlight seemed to come. All ready. (DALE *moves up* L. *at door, ready to turn out stand lamp.* CORNELIA *at door* R.*)* I shall go up this way and down the other. *(Exit* CORNELIA R., *closing door.* DOCTOR *looking up staircase. His face changes, showing surprise and apprehension. He glances back into room, and over to* L. *to see if* DALE *can see him. She cannot. To somebody, evidently at top of stairs, he makes an insistent gesture, "Go back, go back."* DALE *turns out stand lamp up* L. *LIGHTS come down little.* DALE *then walks by the French windows to electric button up* C. *Stands with finger on button; she faces* R. THE UNKNOWN *reaches hand in through the broken pane in French window, turns knob on window, unlocking the window door. Then the window door is pushed inward, evidently to admit a crouching figure. When* UN-KNOWN *is in and behind couch, which he pushes down to make room for his body, he closes the door in window. Only his hand seen during this business. When* UNKNOWN *is on stage, back of settee and window closes,* UNKNOWN *pushes button of signal light cable which runs from Center of window off stage to end·of·stairs off* R. *Small LIGHT on* R. *upper.* CORNELIA *off* R. *upper)* All right! Put out the lights! (DALE *pushes button on wall up* C. *LIGHTS out.* DALE *steps just inside alcove, looks up and off stairs. She leans heavily against the* L. *double door.* CORNELIA *off)* Was it here? *(SPOT focusses on* DOCTOR's *face.* DOCTOR *stands at foot of stairs, looking up.)*

DALE. Come down a little.

DOCTOR. *(To* CORNELIA *with an attempt at jocularity)* I hope you have no weapon.

CORNELIA. *(Off)* How's this? *(LOWER SPOT very slightly.)*

DALE. That's about right.

CORNELIA. *(Off)* Lights please. (DALE *pushes the wall button. SPOT OFF. LIGHTS UP. Foots, Border and Brackets and Lamps full on.* CORNELIA *has evidently left the staircase.* DALE *back into room. She goes down* L.C. *to table* C. DOCTOR *backs into room. He comes down* R.C.)

DALE. *(L. table; sits)* Doctor, I'm so frightened!

DOCTOR. *(Down to her* L.*)* Why, my dear child, because you happened to be in the room when a crime is committed?

DALE. But he has a perfect case against me.

DOCTOR. That's absurd!

DALE. No.

DOCTOR. *You don't mean?*

DALE. *(Horrified)* I *didn't kill* him, but you know the piece of blueprint you found in his hand?

DOCTOR. *(Tensely)* Yes?

DALE. There was another piece—a large piece—I tore it from him just before——

DOCTOR. *(Trying to control his excitement)* Why did you do such a thing?

DALE. Oh, I'll explain that later. It's not safe where it is—Billy may throw it out, or burn it without knowing——

DOCTOR. Let me understand this. The butler has that paper now?

DALE. He doesn't know he has it. It was in one of the rolls that went out on the tray.

DOCTOR. *(Slight pause)* Now don't you worry about it. I'll get it. *(He starts* R., *stops, turns to* DALE*)* But you oughtn't to have it in your possession. *(Comes* L. *a step toward her)* Why not let it be burned?

DALE. *(Startled)* Oh, no! It's important—it's vital!

DOCTOR. The tray is in the dining room?
DALE. Yes.

(DOCTOR *exits* R., *closing door.* UNKNOWN *back of
settee up* L.C., *raises himself, just for a second.
Audience just sees top of his head. Moves settee slightly.* DALE *crosses slowly to fireplace.
Enter* BROOKS R.; *closes door behind him. He
carries two logs of wood for fire.* DALE *turns;
sees him; she comes a few steps* R. BROOKS
crosses front of table C.)

DALE. (*As soon as* BROOKS *is on*) Oh! Things
have gone awfully wrong, haven't they?
BROOKS. Be careful! (*Turns, looks* R. *and around
room; crosses to* L.C.) I don't trust even the furniture in this house tonight. (*Moves to* DALE, *kisses
her, then crosses back of her to fireplace. Raises his
voice very formally*) Miss Van Gorder wishes the
fire kept up! (*Drops the wood, turns back to* DALE,
speaks in undertone) Play up!
DALE. (*Distinctly*) Put some logs on the fire,
please. (*Then, in undertone, facing* R. *away from
him*) Jack, I'm nearly distracted! (BROOKS *drops
the wood at fireplace, and quickly comes up behind
her; puts his arms around her.*)
BROOKS. Dale, pull yourself together. We've got
a fight ahead of us. (*As he releases her and starts
back to fireplace*) These old-fashioned fireplaces eat
up a lot of wood. (*Drops on knees; places wood inside fender.*)
DALE. (*Turns and goes toward him; leans on
arms of armchair, which is between them*) You
know why I sent for Richard Fleming, don't you?
BROOKS. (*On knees, turns and faces her*) Yes—
but who in God's name killed him?
DALE. You don't think it was Billy?
BROOKS. (*Half rises*) More likely the man Lizzie

saw going upstairs. I've been all over the upper floors.

DALE. And nothing?

BROOKS. Nothing. *(Leaning over armchair toward* DALE*)* Dale, do you think that——

DALE. *(Is conscious that someone is coming. To* BROOKS*)* Be careful! (BROOKS *turns to fireplace; works with logs.* CORNELIA *enters* R.; *closes door behind her. She carries her black bag. She sees* BROOKS *at fireplace as soon as she enters. Coming to table* C.*)*

CORNELIA. Well, Mr. Alopecia—Urticaria, Rubeola—otherwise Bailey. (BROOKS *rises with a start; faces her. Stares at her. Look between* DALE *and* BROOKS.*)* I wish you young people would remember that even if hair and teeth have fallen out at sixty the mind still functions. *(She reaches into her black knitting-bag and brings out a cabinet photograph of* BROOKS*)* His photograph—sitting on your dresser! (DALE *crosses over to* L.C., *across table from* COR-NELIA. *To* DALE, *as* CORNELIA *holds out the photo toward her)* And that detective with as many eyes as a potato. Burn it and be quick about it!

DALE. *(Takes photo, but continues to stand facing* CORNELIA. *Then glances at* BROOKS, *and back at* CORNELIA*)* Then—you knew?

CORNELIA. *(Sitting* R. *of table* C.*)* My dear child, I have employed many gardeners in my time, and never before had one who manicured his finger nails, who wore silk socks, who talked like Harvard condescending to Yale—(BROOKS *registers this by looking down)*—and who regards baldness as a plant instead of a calamity. (DALE *crosses to fireplace; throws photo in fire. FLICKER in fireplace.)*

BROOKS. *(At same time crosses to* L.C., *facing* CORNELIA*)* Do you know why I'm here?

CORNELIA. I do—and a pretty mess you've put me in by coming here. If that detective was as smart as he thinks he is, he'd have had you an hour ago. *(She rises, crosses* BROOKS *to* L. *toward* DALE; *then* DALE *becomes very grave.)* Now, I want to ask *you* something. Was there a blueprint and did you get it from Richard Fleming?

DALE. Yes.

BROOKS. *(Facing* CORNELIA *and* DALE*)* Dale! Don't you see where this places you? If you had it, why didn't you give it to Anderson when he asked for it?

CORNELIA. Because she had sense enough to see that Mr. Anderson considered that piece of paper the final link in the evidence against *her!*

BROOKS. But she could have no *motive.*

CORNELIA. Couldn't she? The detective thinks she could—to save you!

BROOKS. *(Takes step back; slight pause)* Good God!

CORNELIA. *(Close to* DALE*)* Where is the paper now?

DALE. The Doctor is getting it for me.

CORNELIA. *What!*

DALE. It was on the tray Billy took out.

CORNELIA. *(Puts hands up, depressed)* Well, I'm afraid everything's over. *(She crosses to front of table* C.*)*

DALE. *(Plaintively, follows to* L.C. BROOKS *at same time crosses* DALE *to* L.*)* I didn't know what else to do.

CORNELIA. *(Looks door* R.*)* One of two things will happen now. Either the Doctor's an honest man, in which case, as Coroner, he will hand that paper to the detective, or he is *not* an honest man, and he will keep it for himself. *I* don't think he's an honest man.

DALE. *(Goes up* L.C.; *meets* CORNELIA *back of table* C.*)* Then you think the Doctor may give the paper to Mr. Anderson?

CORNELIA. He may, or he may not. *(Enter* BILLY R. CORNELIA *takes a step toward* BILLY*)* I want to know the moment *anybody goes upstairs.* I want to know—immediately. (BILLY *is about to go.)* Oh, Billy—— *(She steps up* C., *looks up stairs, then)* Where is the Doctor?

BILLY. In dining room, having cup coffee.

CORNELIA. And Mr. Beresford?

BILLY. Sit on kitchen floor, inside door, with gun. (CORNELIA *motions* BILLY *to go. Exit* BILLY R.*)*

CORNELIA. *(To* DALE*)* Dale, watch that door. *(Indicating door* R. DALE *crosses to door* R.*)* And warn me if anyone is coming. (CORNELIA *goes down to chair* R.I, *gets* DOCTOR's *bag, carries it to table* C., *places on table, up stage end, turns to* BROOKS*)* Get some soot.

BROOKS. *(*L.C.*)* Soot?

CORNELIA. Yes, soot, from the back of that fireplace. (BROOKS *takes envelope from pocket, goes to fireplace, reaches far in, scrapes back of fireplace; envelope blackened. At same time* CORNELIA *steps up* C. *to stand, gets piece of writing paper, places it with lead pencil on table.)*

BROOKS. *(To table)* Is this all right?

CORNELIA. Yes. Now rub it onto the handle of that bag. *(Indicating* DOCTOR's *bag.* BROOKS *blackens the handle.)*

DALE. Somebody's coming! (BROOKS *quickly to fireplace; pretends to work at fireplace.* DALE *goes up* R.C.*)*

CORNELIA. *(Pretending to carry on conversation and carries bag back to chair* R.I. *She does not touch the handle of bag)* We all need sleep and I think—— *(Motions to others.)*

BILLY. *(Enters just inside of door* R.*)* Doctor just go upstairs. *(Exits, leaving door open.)*

CORNELIA. *(Steps to door* R.; *looks off; calls)*
Oh, Doctor! Doctor!

DOCTOR. *(Off* R. *Apparently from stairway)* Yes?
(CORNELIA *back to* R. *down stage. A moment's
pause.* DOCTOR *enters* R.; *he takes a furtive glance
around the room, then down to* R.C. *Faces* CORNE-
LIA; *just about to speak)* Your maid insists that a
man went up that staircase before the crime. I was
going to take a look around.

CORNELIA. *(Pleasantly, down* R.*)* The gardener
has just made a thorough search.

DALE. *(Coming down* R. *of* DOCTOR*)* Doctor, did
you? (DETECTIVE *KNOCKS on terrace door. On
the knock* DOCTOR *moves* C., *half turns, looks up
stage.)*

DETECTIVE. *(Outside on terrace; muffled voice)*
It's Anderson.

BROOKS. *(Crosses up to terrace door)* The detective. *(Unbolts door for* DETECTIVE.*)*

DALE. *(Following* DOCTOR *to* C. *below table* C.*)*
Did you get it?

DOCTOR. (C. *Turns; looks at* DALE*)* My dear
child, are you *sure* you put it there?

DALE. *(Dismayed)* Why, yes, I—— *(She looks
at him; suddenly distrusts him.* DALE *turns; ex-
changes looks with* CORNELIA. BROOKS *stands up
L.C. near window.* DETECTIVE *comes in terrace door,
slams it behind him, comes down* R.C. DOCTOR *over
to* L.*)*

DETECTIVE. *(Stays up in doorway; irritably)* I
couldn't find anybody. I think that Jap's crazy.

DOCTOR. *(Getting coat on, over* L. *from settee)*
Well, I think I've fulfilled all the legal requirements.
I must be going.

DETECTIVE. *(Turns, takes step up* R.C., *faces* DOC-
TOR*)* Doctor, did you ever hear Courtleigh Fleming mention a Hidden Room in this house?

DOCTOR. *(Does not look directly at* DETECTIVE*)* No—and I knew him rather well.

DETECTIVE. You don't think, then, that such a room and the money in it could be the motive of this crime?

DOCTOR. I don't believe Courtleigh Fleming robbed his own bank. If that's what you mean. *(*DOCTOR *crosses above table to* R.I *to get his bag.* DETECTIVE *crosses above table* C. DOCTOR, *to* COR-NELIA*)* Well, I can't wish you a comfortable night, but I can hope it will be a quiet one. *(*DOCTOR *gets bag in right hand, cap in left.)*

CORNELIA. *(Crosses to* DOCTOR. *She goes* R.C. *up to top of table* C. DALE *goes* L.C.*)* We're naturally upset. Perhaps you will write a prescription. Some sleeping medicine.

DOCTOR. Why, certainly. *(He comes toward table.* CORNELIA *hands him paper and pencil. He is about to write on paper, using the bag as a pad.)*

CORNELIA. I hoped you would. Here is paper and pencil.

DOCTOR. *(Taking the paper in right hand)* I don't generally advise these drugs, but—— *(Then stopping short)* What time is it?

CORNELIA. *(Looks at clock on mantel)* Half-past eleven.

DOCTOR. Then I'd better bring you the powders. The pharmacy closes at eleven. *(She takes the paper from* DOCTOR; *puts it down on table* C. *without looking at it. From the blackened handle of the bag his thumb has made a clear impression on the paper. He is quite unconscious of this.* CORNELIA *picks up the paper, with apparent carelessness, glances at it, and lays it with the print down. She picks up a key off table.* DOCTOR *goes* R.*)*

CORNELIA. Dale will let you out, Doctor. *(*DALE *crosses front of table* L. *to* R.C.; *gets key from* COR-NELIA.*)*

DOCTOR. *(Stops, turns, smiles at* CORNELIA*)* That's right. Keep things locked up. Discretion is the better part of valor. (DALE *waits just in* R. *doorway for* DOCTOR.*)*

CORNELIA. *(Up* C.*)* I've been discreet for sixty years, and sometimes I think it was a mistake. (DALE *exits* R. DOCTOR *follows her off.)*

DETECTIVE. *(Looks with angry eye on* BROOKS, *who is up* R.C.*)* I guess we can do without you!

BROOKS. All right, sir. *(Exits* R. *Closes door.)*

DETECTIVE. *(Comes over to table* L.C. *To* COR-NELIA*)* Now, I want a few words with you! *(His tone is surly.)*

CORNELIA. *(*R.C., *beside table* C.*)* Which means that you mean to do all the talking. Very well! But first I want to show you something. Will you come here, please? *(She starts up to alcove.)*

DETECTIVE. I've examined that staircase.

CORNELIA. Not with me! I have something to show you. (DETECTIVE *follows her up. They exit up the staircase. The room is now empty.)*

(LIZZIE *enters* R., *carrying hot-water bottle, filled with sand, and a large butcher knife.* UNKNOWN *opens the door in French windows, up* L.C. *He is getting out of the room by the window, unseen.* LIZZIE, *after closing door* R., *sees the French window move. It closes. She gives a wild screech; drops the water bag on chair above stand, just above door* R. CORNELIA *and* DETECTIVE *run down the stairs. When* LIZZIE *sees them she points at window.* DALE *enters* R.*)*

LIZZIE. *(Wildly)* That window! It closed— without human hands! (CORNELIA *goes up to window* L.C.; *looks out.* DETECTIVE *stands in double door* R.C.; *looks at* LIZZIE.*)*

DETECTIVE. *(Speaks to* CORNELIA, *but looking at* LIZZIE*)* I wish you'd put this screech owl to bed!

LIZZIE. *(Agitatedly)* You'd screech owl yourself if you saw what I saw! (LIZZIE *collapses into chair; sits on water bottle. She gives a scream, jumps up and points to water bottle on chair)* I'm scalded again! I can't walk and now I can't sit. (DETECTIVE *takes her by the shoulder and pushes her off* R. *They exit. Close door.)*

DALE. *(Starting over cautiously to* R.C. *to* CORNELIA*)* It isn't there. The Doctor says he didn't see it and I've looked. It's gone.

CORNELIA. *(Up* R.C.*)* Then the Doctor—— *(She stops; hears doorknob move* R. DALE *back to* R.I; *sits chair. Enter* DETECTIVE R.; *closes door.)*

DETECTIVE. *(*R.C. *to* CORNELIA*)* Now, your point about that thumb-print on the stair rail is very interesting. But just what does it prove?

CORNELIA. *(*C.*)* It points down——

DETECTIVE. It does—and what then?

CORNELIA. It shows that somebody stood there, for some time, listening to my niece and Richard Fleming, in this room below.

DETECTIVE. All right, I'll grant that to save argument, but the moment that shot was fired the lights came on. If somebody on that staircase shot him, and then came down and took the blueprint, Miss Ogden would have seen him. *(He turns to* DALE*)* Did you?

DALE. *(*R.I*)* No, nobody came down.

CORNELIA. *(Takes a step* R.*)* Now, Mr. Anderson——

DETECTIVE. Now, I'm not hounding this girl. I haven't said yet that she committed the murder, but she took that blueprint, and I want it.

CORNELIA. You want it to connect her with the murder.

DETECTIVE. *(Savagely)* It's rather reasonable to

suppose that I might want to return the funds to the Union Bank, isn't it? Provided they're here.

CORNELIA. I see. Well, I'll tell you this much, Mr. Anderson, and I'll ask you to believe me as a gentlewoman, granting that at one time my niece knew something of that blueprint, at this moment we do not know where it is or who has it. *(Crosses to L.C.)*

DETECTIVE. *(R.C.)* Damnation—— *(Mutters)* That's the truth, is it?

CORNELIA. That's the truth. *(She sits L. of table C.; takes out knitting; knits. Pause. To DETECTIVE)* Did you every try knitting when you wanted to think?

DETECTIVE. No. *(He crosses over to table C., takes out cigar, lights it. Matches on table.)*

CORNELIA. You should some time! I find it very helpful!

DETECTIVE. I don't need knitting to think straight! *(Starts to walk up R.C.)*

CORNELIA. I wonder! You seem to have so much evidence left over. (DETECTIVE *turns; looks at her.*) Did you ever hear of the man who took a clock apart, and when he put it together again he had enough left over to make another clock? (DETECTIVE *comes down* R.C., *looking at* DALE. DALE *seated* R.I.)

DETECTIVE. *(Ignoring* CORNELIA. *To* DALE*)* What do you mean by saying that paper isn't where you put it?

CORNELIA. *(Quickly)* She hasn't said that. (DETECTIVE *walks up* R.C., *impatient movement.*) Do you believe in circumstantial evidence?

DETECTIVE. It's my business.

CORNELIA. While you have been investigating, I too have not been idle. (DETECTIVE *gives a mean laugh; crosses* R.C. *again.*) To me it is perfectly obvious that one *intelligence*—(DETECTIVE *stops; looks at* CORNELIA*)*—has been at work, behind many of the things that have occurred in this house.

DETECTIVE. Who?

CORNELIA. I'll ask you that! Some one person who, knowing Courtleigh Fleming well, probably knows of the existence of a Hidden Room in this house—and who, finding us in occupation of the house, has tried to get rid of me in two ways: First by frightening me with anonymous threats, and second, by urging me to leave. Someone who very possibly entered this house tonight, shortly before the murder, and slipped up that staircase.

DETECTIVE. *(Startled)* The Doctor? *(Step down.)*

CORNELIA. *(Still knitting)* When Doctor Wells said he was leaving here earlier in the evening for the Johnsons', he did not go there. He was not expected to go there. I found that out when I telephoned.

DETECTIVE. *(Moves head, eyes narrowing)* The Doctor!

CORNELIA. As you know, I had a supplementary bolt placed on that door. *(Refers to terrace door.)* Earlier this evening Doctor Wells said that he had bolted it when he had left it open, purposely as I now realize, in order that later he might return. You may recall that Doctor Wells took a scrap of paper from Richard Fleming's hand and tried to conceal it. Why did he do *that? (Slight pause; changes tone)* May I ask you to look at this? *(She picks up from the table the paper containing* DOCTOR WELLS' *thumb-print.)*

DETECTIVE. *(Over to table,* R.C.; *takes the paper)* A thumb-print—— *(Looks at it)* Whose is it?

CORNELIA. Doctor Wells'. *(She picks up reading-glass and offers it to* DETECTIVE. *He takes it; looks through it at paper.)* They say thumb-prints never lie.

DETECTIVE. *(Slight pause, looking at paper. Sarcastically)* You don't really think you *need* a detective, do you?

CORNELIA. *(Quietly ironical)* I am a humble follower in your footsteps.

DETECTIVE. *(Ironically bows to her; then she bows)* Well, I'll bite! Anything to help a sister in the profession!

CORNELIA. *(Calmly)* You'll find that the same hand that made that left the imprint on the staircase. (DETECTIVE *looks at* CORNELIA, *then up; goes up to foot of staircase. He turns and surveys the two women, then he goes slowly up the staircase and off* R. DALE *half rises, as if to speak to* CORNELIA. CORNELIA *makes a warning gesture.* DALE *sinks back into chair* R.I.)

BERESFORD. *(Enters* R. *Closes door. Comes* R.C. *Faces* CORNELIA*)* Miss Van Gorder, may I ask you to make an excuse and call your gardener here? (DALE *starts violently.* CORNELIA *betrays no emotion, save that she knits a trifle more rapidly.)*

CORNELIA. The gardener? Certainly—if you'll touch that bell. (BERESFORD *goes up* R.C.; *pushes button on wall; stands there.* DALE *is in an agony of suspense.)*

DETECTIVE. *(Comes quietly down the stairs into the room, down* R.*)* It's no good, Miss Van Gorder. The prints are not the same.

CORNELIA. Not the same!

DETECTIVE. *(Smoking cigar; lays down the reading-glass and paper on table)* If you think I'm mistaken, I'll leave it to any unprejudiced person or your own eyesight. Thumb-prints never lie. Did you ever try a good cigar when you wanted to think?

CORNELIA. I still believe it was the Doctor.

DETECTIVE. And yet the Doctor was in this room tonight, according to your own statement, when the anonymous letter came through the window. (BILLY *enters* R.)

BERESFORD. *(Steps down a little and to* R.; *to* BILLY*)* Tell the gardener Miss Van Gorder wants him—and don't say we're all here. (BILLY *exits* R.)

DETECTIVE. *(Up* C.; *to* BERESFORD, *rather grimly)* I seem to have plenty of *help* in this case!

DALE. *(Rises; to* BERESFORD*)* Why have you sent for the gardener?

BERESFORD. *(Grimly)* I'll tell you that in a moment. (DALE *crosses below table to* L. *Enter* BROOKS R.; *takes a swift survey of the room; closes door. Slight pause.)*

BROOKS. *(To* CORNELIA*)* You sent for me?

BERESFORD. *(Up* R.C. *With eye on* BROOKS, *speaks to* CORNELIA *brusquely)* How long has this man been in your employ?

CORNELIA. *(Still seated* L. *of table* C.*)* Why does that interest you?

BROOKS. I came this evening.

BERESFORD. Exactly. *(To* DETECTIVE, *who stands up* C.*)* I've been trying to recall this man's face ever since I came tonight—I know now who it is.

DETECTIVE. Who is he?

BROOKS. *(Straightening)* It's all right, Beresford. I know you think you're doing your duty, but I wish to God you could have *restrained* your sense of duty for about three hours more.

BERESFORD. To let you get away?

BROOKS. No—to let me finish what I came here to do.

BERESFORD. Don't you think you've done enough? *(Turns to* DETECTIVE*)* This man has imposed on the credulity of these women. I am quite sure, without their knowledge. His name is Bailey, of the Union Bank.

DETECTIVE. *(Puts cigar on ashtray. To* BROOKS*)* That's the truth, is it?

BROOKS. It's true, all right.

BERESFORD. I accuse him not only of the thing he is wanted for but of the murder of Richard Fleming.

BROOKS. *(Fiercely to* BERESFORD*)* You lie!

DETECTIVE. *(Turns; goes down a step toward* DALE*)* You knew this? *(Turns to* CORNELIA*)* Did you?

CORNELIA. Yes.

DETECTIVE. Then it's a conspiracy, is it? All this case against the Doctor! *(Wheels on* BROOKS*)* What did you mean by that—"three hours more"?

BROOKS. I could have cleared myself in three hours. *(DOORBELL rings off* R.*)*

CORNELIA. *(*L.C.*)* Probably the Doctor. He was to come back with some sleeping-powders. *(Enter* BILLY R. *He goes to table, upper end* C.; *gets key.)*

DETECTIVE. *(To* BILLY*)* If that's the Doctor, admit him. If it's anybody else, call me. (BILLY *exits* R.; *leaves door open. To* BROOKS*)* Have you got a gun on you?

BROOKS. No.

DETECTIVE. I'll just make sure of that. *(Crosses to* BROOKS. BERESFORD *crosses above table to* L.C., *above chair.* DETECTIVE *turns* BROOKS *to face* R.; *frisks* BROOKS; *then takes pair handcuffs out of pocket and puts them on table* C.*)*

DALE. *(At sight of handcuffs, over* L.*)* Oh, no! I can't bear it! I'll tell you everything. (ALL *the characters turn and face* DALE. DOCTOR *enters* R., *leaving the door open behind him. In the intensity of the scene the* DOCTOR'S *entrance is ignored.* DALE *continues)* He got to the foot of the staircase— Richard Fleming, I mean. *(To* DETECTIVE*)* And he had the blueprint you've been talking about. I had told him Jack Bailey was here as the gardener, and he said if I screamed he would tell that. I was desperate—I threatened him with the revolver, but he took it from me. Then I tore the blueprint from him—he was shot—from the stairs.

BERESFORD. *(Up back of chair* L.C.*)* By Bailey!

BROOKS. *(Strong; over* R.*)* I didn't even know he was in the house.

DETECTIVE. What did you do with the blueprint? *(*DOCTOR *is listening intently.)*

DALE. I put it first in the neck of my dress—then, when I found you were watching me, I hid it, somwhere else. *(She glances over at the* DOCTOR. *He is apprehensive and anxious. It is evident that he would make his escape, but* BILLY *at that moment enters with key.)*

BILLY. Key—front door. *(He crosses in front of* DOCTOR *and behind the* OTHER CHARACTERS *to table, upper end; places key there, and exits* R.*)*

DALE. *(Does not wait for this business)* I put it —somewhere else. *(Again she glances at* DOCTOR.*)*

DETECTIVE. Did you give it to Bailey?

DALE. No—I hid it, and then I told where it was —to the Doctor. *(*ALL *turn in surprise to* DOCTOR, *who is at door* R. CORNELIA *rises.)*

DOCTOR. *(Smiles grimly, then slowly comes down into scene* R.*)* That's rather inaccurate. You told me where you had placed it, but when I went to look for it it was gone.

CORNELIA. *(*L.C. *Strongly)* Are you quite sure of that?

DOCTOR. *(Gaining courage)* Absolutely. *(Then to* DETECTIVE*)* She said she had hidden it inside one of the rolls that were on the tray. *(He crosses to table* C., *front of the* OTHERS, *takes out a box of powders from overcoat pocket and places them on table)* On that table. She was in such distress that I finally agreed to look for it—it wasn't there.

DETECTIVE. *(Has come down* R. *behind the* DOCTOR. *To* DOCTOR*)* Did you realize the significance of this paper?

DOCTOR. *(Turns to* DETECTIVE*)* Nothing beyond the fact that Miss Ogden was afraid it linked her with the crime.

DETECTIVE. *(Considers a moment, then to* COR-NELIA*)* I'd like to have a few minutes with the Doctor alone.

(CORNELIA *and* DALE *cross front of table toward door* R. CORNELIA *with arm around* DALE, *upstage side.* BROOKS *stands below door* R. *As* DALE *passes him she puts out her hand to him.* BROOKS *grasps* DALE'S *hand. Exit* CORNELIA *and* DALE R.*)*

DETECTIVE. *(As* CORNELIA *and* DALE *are crossing to* R.*)* Beresford, take Bailey to the library and see that he stays there.

(DOCTOR *has crossed to* L.; *takes off his overcoat and places it on settee up* L.C. BROOKS *and* BERES-FORD *exit* R. BERESFORD *closes the door behind them.* DETECTIVE *up to doors* R.C.; *closes them; then he comes down a few steps, facing the* DOCTOR, *who stands over* L.C., *up stage.)*

DETECTIVE. Now, Doctor, I'll have that blueprint.

DOCTOR. *(Eyeing him warily)* I've just made the statement that I didn't find that blueprint.

DETECTIVE. *(Dryly)* I heard you! Now, this situation is between you and me, Doctor Wells—it has nothing to do with that poor fool of a cashier. He didn't take that money and you know it. It's in this house, and you know that too.

DOCTOR. In this house?

DETECTIVE. In this house! Tonight when you claimed to be making a professional call, you were in this house—and I think you were on that staircase when Richard Fleming was killed!

DOCTOR. No, Anderson, I'll swear I was not.

DETECTIVE. I'll tell you something. *(Steps up* R.C.*)* Miss Van Gorder very cleverly got a thumbprint of yours tonight. Does that mean anything to you?

DOCTOR. Nothing. I have not been upstairs in this house in three months. *(Up to this point he is obviously telling the truth.* DETECTIVE *is puzzled.)*

DETECTIVE. Before Courtleigh Fleming died, did he tell you anything about a Hidden Room—in this house?

DOCTOR. *(His air of honesty lessens; he becomes furtive)* No.

DETECTIVE. You haven't been trying to frighten those women out of here with anonymous letters so you could get in?

DOCTOR. No—certainly not. *(Slight pause.* DETECTIVE *walks down sideways* R.*)*

DETECTIVE. Let me see your keyring?

*(*DOCTOR *unwillingly produces keyring.* DETECTIVE *over few steps to* C. DOCTOR *steps* R. *and hands out keys to* DETECTIVE, *who takes them.* DETECTIVE, *with revolver in hand, goes up into alcove, unlocks terrace door, goes out, leaving terrace door open.* DOCTOR *glances upstage to see if* DETECTIVE *is out of sight. He gets piece of blueprint out of his pocket and tiptoes to the fireplace with it. He throws paper toward grate, but it falls on floor outside of grate. A flash of LIGHTNING reveals through the broken pane in window* DETECTIVE, *who is on terrace, and has drawn the shade aside. Slight rumble of THUNDER, LIGHTNING, while* DETECTIVE *on terrace looking through window.)*

DETECTIVE. *(Sees* DOCTOR *throw the paper to floor; with noiseless swiftness the* DETECTIVE *is back in the room, and has the* DOCTOR *covered with revolver. Up* R.C.*)* Pick that up. (DOCTOR *does pick it up.)* And put it on the table. (DOCTOR *slowly to table with paper.)* Now—stand away from the table—— (DOCTOR *backs away to* L.C. *up stage. A low rumble of THUNDER. LIGHTNING.* DETECTIVE *lowers revolver, puts keys on table and stands back of table* C., *looking at the blueprint. Lays the revolver on table,* R. *side, upper end. Looks up at* DOCTOR *with a half-sardonic smile, then examining blueprint)* Behind a fireplace, eh? What fireplace? In what room?

DOCTOR. *(Up* L.C. *Sullenly)* I won't tell you!

DETECTIVE. *(Above table* C.*)* All right. I'll find it, you now. *(Consulting blueprint again, leaning over table.)*

(DOCTOR *maintains a furious silence; now stands with back to audience, up* L.C. *Slight pause. Then with a leap the* DOCTOR *is on top of the* DETECTIVE. *There follows a silent, furious struggle.* DOCTOR *pins* DETECTIVE'S *arms behind him.* DETECTIVE *bends down; gets his right arm free; gets revolver off table, but he drops it to floor. Then* DOCTOR *gets* DETECTIVE'S *both arms pinned behind him, and reaches back to stand up* C. *and gets hold of the telephone.* (NOTE: *Phone of Act I replaced by property all-rubber phone.)* DOCTOR *hits the* DETECTIVE *over the head with base of phone, rendering* DETECTIVE *insensible. THUNDER, LIGHTNING, WIND.* DETECTIVE *falls over* L., *upstage, his head toward door* L.3. DOCTOR *straightens up; listens tensely. There is no sound from the rest of the house. Only the thunder and lightning.* DOCTOR *picks up the revolver, puts in pocket, gets the blue-*

*print, puts in pocket. Now gets down on his
knees below* DETECTIVE. *Rapidly gags him.*
NOTE: *A very efficient gag can be made by tying several hard knots in the middle of a handkerchief, forcing the knots into the mouth, and
then tying the ends of the handkerchief behind
the head.* DOCTOR *then takes his own muffler
and raps it around head of* DETECTIVE. *After
the handkerchief gag is on,* DOCTOR *listens and
looks* R. *and* L., *then he gets the handcuffs off
the table, left there in scene with* BROOKS. DOC-
TOR *now locks the handcuffs on* DETECTIVE'S
*wrists; not behind his back, but in front of him.
Then he puts arms under* DETECTIVE'S *arms and
drags* DETECTIVE *off* L.3. *Comes into the room
again. Closes and locks door* L.3. *And then
cautiously crosses up stage to* R. *He starts to
go up into alcove,* R.C. *He makes a dash for the
staircase. There is a KNOCK on terrace door
behind him. He backs down quickly, looks at
door where the knocks came from. Backs into
room. Then he is about to start up into alcove
again when* BERESFORD *enters from* R. *below
staircase. Goes to terrace door.* BERESFORD
looks at DOCTOR. DOCTOR *points at door, and
backs into room.* DOCTOR *goes* L.C. *upstage.)*

BERESFORD. *(Four KNOCKS. Speaking through
the door)* Who's that? *(No answer.* BERESFORD
draws revolver from pocket. THE UNKNOWN, *outside terrace door, repeats KNOCKS on terrace
door. All the other characters now enter door* R.
CORNELIA, LIZZIE, DALE, BROOKS *and* BILLY. BILLY
closes door R. *behind him.)*
CORNELIA. *(As she enters and goes up toward
doors* R.C.; *sees* BERESFORD*)* What was that noise?
DOCTOR. Someone at that door.
BERESFORD. *(Still in alcove at door)* Sh! **Sh!**

Shall I open it? *(THUNDER, WIND, LIGHT-NING throughout this scene.* CORNELIA, *up to double doors; stands* R.C.*)*

LIZZIE. *(With a low wail)* If it ain't human, it's dead! If it *is* human, we're dead! *(Four KNOCKS repeated by* UNKNOWN.*)*

CORNELIA. *(Up* R.C.*)* Be careful, Mr. Beresford.

LIZZIE. *(Moans)* It's The Bat!

*(*BERESFORD *very cautiously opens the terrace door. As he does so—clap of THUNDER, WIND, LIGHTNING, LIGHTS BLINK. At the same moment* UNKNOWN, *who has been leaning against the terrace door, falls into* BERESFORD'S *arms.* BERESFORD *drops his revolver and catches the man so he does not fall to floor in alcove.* UNKNOWN *straightens up himself, achieves a certain measure of action and balances himself; staggers into room.* UNKNOWN *is rather good looking. It is seen that there is dried blood on his forehead. His feet and hands have been tied, and pieces of rope still dangle from his wrists and ankles.* UNKNOWN *staggers* L., *above table.* DOCTOR *on upper and* L. *side of him.* BERESFORD *on* R. *side. When clear of the table and* L.C., UNKNOWN *gives a couple of steps forward and falls prone on his face, well down* L.C.*)*

BERESFORD. *(Beneath his breath)* Good God!

CORNELIA. *(Comes down* R.C. *General movement when* UNKNOWN *fell)* Doctor!

(THUNDER and LIGHTNING and WIND die out. DOCTOR *stoops down over prostrate man, turns him over, puts hand over heart.* CORNELIA R.C. DALE *and* LIZZIE R. *of her.* BILLY R. BROOKS *up* C., *back of table.)*

DOCTOR. *(L.)* He's fainted! Struck on the head, too.

CORNELIA. Who is it?

DOCTOR. I never saw him before. Does anyone recognize him? (ALL *look at* UNKNOWN. *Slight pause. No one recognizes him.*)

CORNELIA. Is he badly hurt?

DOCTOR. It's hard to say. I think not. (UNKNOWN *moves, and makes effort to sit up.* BERESFORD *and* DOCTOR *assist him. He gets to his feet. He sways.*) A chair—— (BROOKS *quickly steps forward from table and places the chair that is* L. *of table more* L.C. UNKNOWN *collapses into chair.*) You're all right now, my friend. *(In professional, cheerful voice)* Dizzy a bit, aren't you?

UNKNOWN. *(Makes no answer, stretches his arms, rubs his wrists)* Water!

CORNELIA. *(To* BILLY*)* Bring some water. (BILLY *crosses* R.)

DOCTOR. Whiskey would be better.

CORNELIA. Billy! (BILLY *stops and turns.*) There's whiskey in my room.

BILLY. *(Brightening)* Yes—hid in closet—I know. (CORNELIA *stares at him. He exits* R.C. *and goes up and off by stairs.*)

DOCTOR. *(To* UNKNOWN*)* Now, my man, you're in the hands of friends. Brace up.

BERESFORD. Where's Anderson? (UNKNOWN *starts, then controls himself. From this point on it is evident to the audience that the* UNKNOWN *is not as dazed as he seems to be.*) This is a police matter. *(Makes a movement* L., *as if to go.*)

DOCTOR. *(Raises hand to stop* BERESFORD*)* He was here a moment ago. He'll be back presently. *(Gives* UNKNOWN *a little shake)* Rouse yourself, man! What has happened to you?

UNKNOWN. *(Slowly and apparently with difficulty)* I'm dazed—I don't remember!

CORNELIA. What a night! *(Front of table; turns to* DALE, R.C.*)* Richard Fleming murdered in this house—and now—this! (UNKNOWN *is sitting well down stage* L.C., *so that his face is visible to the audience but not to those on the stage. He gives a swift, stealthy glance at* CORNELIA, *Then his eyes fall again.)*

DALE. Why doesn't somebody ask him his name? (BROOKS *crosses from above table to* R. *of* UN-KNOWN.*)*

BERESFORD. Where the devil is that detective? *(He rushes off* R. *Leaves door open.)*

BROOKS. *(To* UNKNOWN*)* What's your name? (UNKNOWN *makes no reply.)*

CORNELIA. Look at his papers. (BROOKS *looks in his pockets,* UNKNOWN'S R. *side.* DOCTOR, L. *side. Trousers only. He has no coat or vest on. Slight pause.)*

BROOKS. Not a paper on him.

(GLASS CRASH off R., *supposed to be at head of stairs.* BERESFORD *rushes on from* R. *up to* R. *and* L. *of double doors; stands.* ALL *turn up; look at the doors up* R.C., *except the* UNKNOWN, *who half rises in his chair. Tense and alert.* BILLY, *terrified, backs down the small staircase and into the room. He stands with his back to the audience, a rigid little figure, with horror in every outline.)*

CORNELIA. *(Sharply)* Billy!
DALE. Billy! What is it?
BILLY. *(Moistens his dry lips with his tongue)* It—nothing. (UNKNOWN *sinks back into his chair, and resumes his pose of immobility.)*

BERESFORD. *(Crosses and catches* BILLY *by the shoulders; swings* BILLY *round to face him)* Now, see here! You've seen something! What was it?

BILLY. *(Trembling)* Ghost! Ghost!

CORNELIA. He's concealing something. Look at him!

BILLY. No! No! No! (BERESFORD *releases* BILLY *and steps back and up* R.C.)

CORNELIA. *(Over* R. *and looking up* R.C. *To* BROOKS)* Brooks, close that door. *(Points up at terrace door in alcove.* BROOKS *quickly up into alcove. Terrace door is SLAMMED shut in his face. At same time LIGHTS out. All dark.)*

BROOKS. *(In alcove)* This door's locked—the key's gone. *(To* BERESFORD)* Where's your revolver, Beresford? *(Goes* L., *above* C. *table.)*

BERESFORD. I dropped it, in the alcove.

CORNELIA. I have one. Quick, there's a candle on the table. Light it, somebody!

BERESFORD. *(To* L. *of table, quickly)* Righto! *(He tricks LIGHT in his wrist watch on.* LIZZIE *sees wrist watch light; points at it.)*

LIZZIE. The eye! The eye! *(Meanwhile* BERESFORD *has struck match and lighted candle.)*

(ELECTRICIAN comes up on candle light in strip, foots and border. LIZZIE *and* BILLY *back away toward door* R. *to get out.* BROOKS *has come down to door* R.)*

BROOKS. This door's locked.

(NOTE: *As soon as* BROOKS *comes down, from alcove, property man tacks the paper BAT to the double door that opens off* R. *Doors* R.C. *closed.)*

CORNELIA. *(Taking the candle off table* C., *and revolver)* I know there's somebody upstairs. We'll go this way. *(She starts up* R. *to* C. OTHERS *all turn and take a step toward double doors.* BROOKS *up to doors* R.C. *Doors are closed and locked.)*

BROOKS. Locked!

CORNELIA. *(Holds up the lighted candle) A Bat!*

(Black paper Bat is tacked to the door R.C. THE UNKNOWN *rises and stands looking up at doors* R.C. ALL THE CHARACTERS *are facing up toward* R.C. *doors.)*

CURTAIN

ACT THREE

Scene: *The trunk room on the third floor.*

The walls of room, except fireplace up Center, window L.2 and door down R.1, are lined with high closets, with practical doors in each. Up C. rear, a wooden fireplace (mantel).

Instead of the grate, there is an iron fireplate fastened in, making the mantel, when it moves, as solid as a door. Mantelpiece swings open on concealed hinges, revealing behind it a room, perhaps 6 feet by 6, in which is a tall iron safe. The mantel is opened by pushing aside a panel in a row of drawers. Up L.C. and left of the mantel, revealing a knob which, when turned, swings the mantel out like a door.

Down R. is a large wicker hamper. Right of this two small old battered trunks. Set up and down stage, one on top of the other, R.C. Next to hamper, a kitchen chair without back.

Over L. a kitchen chair with back. Two old boxes up stage R.2 behind door. Some paper bundles up on high shelf above closets up R. Old sewing-machine over Left against wall. A box pin-hinged to set below the casement window, for characters to step on, getting in and out of window. Two old dress-suit cases, to dress scene. Important: Woman's satchel, on floor, front of hamper; matches on top of trunk.

At Rise: *Stage dark, BLUE LIGHT on window.*

Discovered: Masked Man (Detective) *at safe, up stage, Center, back of the open mantelpiece.*

95

He is working at the knob of safe. After a moment MASKED MAN *swings open the safe. He takes out the money-bag, shuts safe, blows out the candle on floor beside safe, shuts off his pocket flash, and closes the mantel.*

Remote HAMMERING heard off R. MASKED MAN *to door* R., *about to open door. CRASH of splintering wood heard off* R. *AD LIB. off* R.

BERESFORD. *(Off* R.*)* You go this way. I'll go that.

BROOKS. *(Off* R.*)* Have your revolver ready.

(During this ad lib. MASKED MAN *darts back, drops the money-bag into hamper* R.C., *and closes lid of hamper. He runs to window, over* L.2. *Gets out of window; goes up ladder below window, up onto the roof. FOOTSTEPS heard coming up stairs off* R. *Door flung open* R., BROOKS *rushes on, stands a second, then runs to window* L.2.*)*

CORNELIA. *(Suddenly enters* R. *with revolver and dead candle)* Hands up—or I'll shoot!

BROOKS. *(Is seen silhouetted against window* L. *He turns, faces* CORNELIA, *throws up his hands)* Don't shoot! It's Bailey!

CORNELIA. *(To front of trunk* R.C.*)* What brought you up here? *(She lights candle.)*

(ELECTRICIAN comes up on strip (No. 2) in foots. For one candle.)

BROOKS. The others will search downstairs. But, Miss Van Gorder, you mustn't run over the house by yourself. Don't you realize that the man who **locked** us in was probably The Bat?

(ELECTRICIAN follows movements of candle with strips in foots.)

CORNELIA. *(Crosses to L.)* That's why I'm running! Anyway, where would a body *be* safe? When eight of us could be locked up together in one room and have to break out, it's a pretty kettle of fish!

BROOKS. That window's open.

CORNELIA. It's a good forty feet to the ground.

BROOKS. *(R.C.; looks around room)* Well, he isn't here. I'll take a look over the rest of this floor. *(He gets to door R.)*

CORNELIA. *(Suddenly looks at floor, and sees candle grease, near window)* Candle grease! *(BROOKS stops, turns and looks at CORNELIA. CORNELIA touches the grease on floor with finger)* Fresh candle grease! *(Goes L.)* Now, who do you suppose did that? Do you remember how Mr. Gillette, in Sherlock Holmes—when he——— *(Voice trails off; she stoops down, follows the candle grease marks to fireplace up C.)* It leads straight to the fireplace. *(She stands erect and surveys the mantel up C.)* It's been going through my mind for half an hour that no chimney flue runs up this side of the house.

BROOKS. Then why the fireplace?

CORNELIA. That's what I'm going to find out?

DALE. *(Off R.)* Jack! Jack! *(Cautiously.)*

(CORNELIA raps on mantel.)

BROOKS. *(Crosses over R.; beckons DALE, who enters)* Come in——— Lock the door behind you. *(BROOKS back to R.C. up stage. DALE closes and locks door R.)* Where are the others?

DALE. *(Up R.)* They're searching the house. There's no sign of anybody.

BROOKS. *(Up R.C.)* Where's Anderson?

DALE. *(Crosses to* R.C.*)* I haven't seen him.

CORNELIA. *(Up* C. *at mantel; raps on wall above mantel with her revolver)* Hollow as Lizzie's head. *(She carefully examines the painted small drawers* L. *of mantel)* Some of these ought to slide or push or something. *(She works practical small drawer. It slides slowly to* R. *(panel), revealing a white door-knob behind the panel)* Merciful powers! It's moving! (DALE *backs away to* R.*, down stage.)*

BROOKS. *(Up to* CORNELIA*)* Give me the revolver, and stand back. (BROOKS *backs down* C. COR-NELIA *backs down to* L. *Pause.* BROOKS *up to the open panel; turns the knob. CUE to pull attached cords to mantel. It opens slowly, swinging* L. *and up against back flat,* L.C. BROOKS *steps down* R.*; faces mantel as it moves.)*

DALE. Look! *(The black aperture of room beyond revealed.* BROOKS *takes candle from* CORNELIA *and revolver; goes up.)*

(ELECTRICIAN follow candle, and as BROOKS *goes into the small room back of mantel up* C.*, DIM OUT. Leaves stage dark.)*

DALE. (BROOKS *gets well up* C.*)* Jack! Be careful!

BROOKS. *(Goes in. A pause)* Nobody home! *(Then triumphantly)* Money! money! We've got the money! *(Stoops, turns lever and opens safe. Stands a moment. Comes out of safe with candle.)*

(ELECTRICIAN catch candle, coming up I *candle light.* BROOKS *comes down* C.*)*

CORNELIA. Well!

BROOKS. The safe's empty—— *(For a moment no one speaks, their disappointment is so great.)*

The money's gone. Well, that settles me! *(With forced laugh.)*

CORNELIA. *(Over to him. She takes candle from him)* Nonsense! The location of this room—the presence of that safe—is enough to establish the facts.

DALE. *(R.C.)* Jack, get Mr. Anderson and show him. *(Violent HAMMERING on door* R. *and a loud scream from* LIZZIE *off* R.*)*

LIZZIE. *(Hysterically off* R.*)* Let me in! For the love of Heaven, let me in! *(*BROOKS *runs* R., *unlocks and opens the door.* LIZZIE *staggers in, her candle hanging down in her hand. ELECTRICIAN catches the light of her candle as she enters in strip* R. *in foots. Almost immediately she gives a cry, and candle goes out. Candle light burns her. Her movement puts it out.)*

CORNELIA. *(L.C.)* Good Heavens, what's the matter?

LIZZIE. *(Over* R., *front of hamper; hysterically)* I saw him! I saw The Bat! He dropped through that skylight out there—*(Points* R.*)*—and run along the hall. He was eight feet tall and he had a face like a demon.

BROOKS. Did you see his face?

LIZZIE. No, he didn't have any face. He was all black where his face ought to be. *(Starts over* L.C.*)*

DALE. A mask!

LIZZIE. *(Crosses over toward* DALE, L.; *volubly)* Yes'm, that's what it was, a mask! *(*BROOKS, *followed by* CORNELIA, *has started for the door* R. *He carries* CORNELIA'S *revolver.* CORNELIA *carries the lighted candle. ELECTRICIAN follows the movement of candle in foots.* LIZZIE *turns; sees* CORNELIA *going toward door* R.; *steps quickly after* CORNELIA*)* Where are you going, Miss Neillie? *(*BROOKS *stands at open door, waiting for* CORNELIA.*)*

CORNELIA. *(Turns to* LIZZIE*)* Keep quiet and don't stick to me like a porous-plaster.

LIZZIE. It's not you I'm sticking to, it's the candle!

CORNELIA. *(To* LIZZIE, *as* CORNELIA *starts for door* R.*)* Go back and stay with Miss Dale *(*CORNELIA *and* BROOKS *exit* R. *with lighted candle. LIGHTS OUT. Room in darkness.)*

DALE. *(*L.C.*)* Lizzie, give me your candle and the matches. *(*LIZZIE *crosses over to* DALE; *gives her the candle and matches.)*

LIZZIE. *(Terrified)* I won't stay here and be murdered in the dark. *(Starts for door* R.*)* If I've got to die, I want to see myself do it! *(She bolts out* R.; *closes door after her.)*

*(*DALE *tries to light candle, striking matches on box. They do not light. To have this business seen, ELECTRICIAN brings up strip in foots* L.C. *just a little. Slight pause.* DALE *looks around the room, then door* R. *very slowly opens about an inch. At first a thread of LIGHT from flashlight gradually widening, then it is extinguished.* DALE *sees this. She is frightened. She darts up to hidden room, goes in and closes the two iron doors noiselessly. STRIP OUT. All dark.* MASKED MAN, *overcoat on, large flash, opens door* R. *very slowly; backs in; flash off. Sweeps room with flashlight. It is the man who was discovered at safe, opening of the Act. He locks the door* R. *Goes to hamper* R.C.; *puts flash for a moment on satchel, front of hamper; picks satchel up; empties its contents into the hamper (old clothes and two paper-backed novels); thrusts the bag of money into satchel; uses flash; works with feverish haste; closes the grip; turns to go to door; hears FOOTSTEPS off* R. *He uses flash sparingly.*

*With satchel in hand, he starts for the window
L.2. As he nears the window, extension ladder
comes up and leans against the window. He
drops the satchel up stage above window. He
is plainly trapped. He darts for the mantel
room; closes the mantel behind him. There is
absolute silence. Pause. Then the ladder
moves as someone climbs it. Stealthily a* MAN'S
SILHOUETTE (DOCTOR) *is seen outside. The*
FIGURE *on the ladder, as he is about to step
through the window into the room, is heard to
hiss cautiously.)*

DOCTOR. Ssssssst! *(Receiving no reply, with infinite caution he crawls in through window. Then
he goes* C. *and starts up for mantel; uses flash—off
—on)* Ssst! *(DOORKNOB* R. *heard turning.*
DOCTOR *starts.)*

BROOKS. *(Off* R.*)* Dale!

CORNELIA. *(Off* R.*)* Dale! Dale! The door's
locked——

BROOKS. *(Off* R.*)* Dale! *(*BROOKS *rattles the
knob; pounds on door; tries to break in.)*

DOCTOR. *(After a moment)* Wait a moment! *(He
goes to door; unlocks it.* BROOKS *hurls himself into
room; crosses* DOCTOR *to* C. *He is followed by* COR-
NELIA *with candle.* LIZZIE *stands in doorway.*
ELECTRICIAN *comes up* I *candle light in foots.)*

BROOKS. *(Turns on* DOCTOR, *who stands* R.C.*)*
Why did you lock that door? *(*BROOKS *takes a look
around the room, and realizes the amazing fact that*
DALE *is not there.)*

DOCTOR. But I didn't.

BROOKS. *(Turns on* DOCTOR*)* You—you——
Where is Miss Ogden? What have you done with
her? *(*CORNELIA *up above hamper* R.C.*)*

DOCTOR. Done with her! I don't know what
you're talking about. I haven't seen her.

BROOKS. *(Threateningly)* You didn't lock that door?

DOCTOR. Absolutely not. I was coming through the window when I heard your voice at the door.

LIZZIE. *(In doorway R., in shaking tones)* In at the window, just like a bat! (CORNELIA *places candle and revolver on hamper. She is facing up C.)*

DOCTOR. I saw lights up here from outside, and I thought——

CORNELIA. *(Interrupting)* That mantel's closed.

DOCTOR. *(Starts as he discovers their knowledge of the Hidden Room)* Damn!

BROOKS. *(To* DOCTOR*)* Did you close it?

DOCTOR. No!!

BROOKS. *(As he starts up to mantel)* I'll see whether you closed it or not. *(Leans against mantel; speaks loud)* Dale! Dale!

*(*DOCTOR *turns front of hamper, back to audience. Picks up the candle from hamper where* COR-NELIA *placed it.* BROOKS *starts to open mantel. As it begins to swing out,* DOCTOR *deliberately extinguishes candle. LIGHTS OUT. Dark stage.* DOCTOR *drops the candle to floor, front of hamper.* MASKED MAN *rushes out of hidden room, back of hamper, to door R. Bumps* LIZZIE *in doorway. She falls to stage, as* MASKED MAN *exits R.* CORNELIA *is up C.)*

CORNELIA. *(As the lights go out)* Doctor, why did you put out that candle?

DOCTOR. I didn't—I——

CORNELIA. You did—I saw you do it. *(DOOR SLAMS.)*

BROOKS. *(Down C.)* What was that?

LIZZIE. *(On floor at doorway)* Oh! Oh! Somebody knocked me down and tramped on me.

CORNELIA. *(Above hamper* R.C.*)* Matches—quick! Where's the candle?

DOCTOR. *(Front of hamper)* Awfully sorry. I assure you it dropped out of the holder. *(Stoops down; gets candle)* Here it is! (BROOKS *to* DOCTOR; *strikes match; lights candle as* DOCTOR *holds it.)*

(ELECTRICIAN come up I *candle effect in foots.* CORNELIA *takes the candle after* BROOKS *lights it.* BROOKS *up to Hidden Room.* DALE *is seen on floor in Hidden Room, in front of the safe.* BROOKS *carries* DALE *down to chair* L. DALE'S *eyes closed.)*

BROOKS. *(As he comes out of Hidden Room with* DALE*)* Doctor! (DOCTOR *crosses to chair over* L.; *feels* DALE'S *pulse.* CORNELIA *holds up candle.)*

CORNELIA. Lizzie, get some whiskey.

LIZZIE. *(As she gets up off floor)* Oh, Miss Neillie, I can't stand any more of this. My spine's driven clean up through my brains.

CORNELIA. *(Going* L.C. *with candle)* You haven't got any spine and you haven't got any brains! Get that whiskey. *(ELECTRICIAN follow movement of candle.* LIZZIE *turns to go out door* R.; *sees* DETECTIVE *in doorway.* DETECTIVE *a grim and menacing figure. He carries a lighted candle.)*

LIZZIE. *(Facing* DETECTIVE *in doorway)* That's right! Come in when everything's over. (DETECTIVE *steps in, and* LIZZIE *exits. ELECTRICIAN catch his candle. Foots* R. 2 *candle light effect now on stage.)*

DOCTOR. *(With back turned toward* DETECTIVE, *facing* L., *looking at* DALE*)* She'll be all right in a moment.

DETECTIVE. *(To* DOCTOR*)* You took my revolver from me downstairs. *(Places lighted candle on trunk,* R. *of hamper; crosses to* L.C. DOCTOR *turns* *and faces him.)* I'll trouble you for it. *(The* OTHERS *are startled.* DOCTOR *sullenly gives up revolver to* DETECTIVE, *who examines and puts it in his hip pocket)* I've something to settle with you, pretty soon, and I'll settle good and proper. *(Crosses below* DOCTOR, *to* L., *over to* DALE*)* Now what's this? *(Indicating* DALE. *Meanwhile* DOCTOR *walks slowly and quietly toward door* R.*)*

CORNELIA. *(A little upstage* L.C.*)* She's coming to. We found her shut in there, Mr. Anderson. *(Indicating hidden room.* DETECTIVE *goes up* C.; *looks at open Hidden Room. As* DOCTOR *is about to exit* R., DETECTIVE *turns; sees* DOCTOR.*)*

DETECTIVE. Wells! *(*CORNELIA *and* BROOKS *work over* DALE. BROOKS *rubs her hands; he is* L. *of her.* CORNELIA *is above* DALE. DOCTOR *stops and turns; faces* DETECTIVE. DETECTIVE *up* C., *then comes down a few steps* C.; *faces* DOCTOR*)* Where were you when she was locked in this room? *(Points up at Hidden Room.)*

DOCTOR. *(Front of hamper,* R.C.*)* I didn't shut her in—if that's what you mean! *(Takes a step toward* C.*)* There was someone shut in there— *(Points up at Hidden Room)*—with her. Ask these people here. *(Indicating* CORNELIA *and* BROOKS *over* L.*)*

CORNELIA. *(Angry)* The fact remains, Doctor, that we left her here alone. When we came back you were here. That door was locked. *(Indicates door* R.*)* And she was in that room. *(*DETECTIVE *goes in Hidden Room. Indicates Hidden Room up* C. *Pause.* CORNELIA *up with candle)* —unconscious! As we opened that door—*(Indicates mantel)*—the Doctor deliberately extinguished the candle.

DETECTIVE. *(Up* C., *wheeling on* DOCTOR; *comes down a step.* CORNELIA *comes down* L.C.*)* Do you know who was in that room?

DOCTOR. *(Sullenly)* No—I didn't put out the

candle. It fell. And I didn't lock that door. *(Indicates door* R.*)* I found it locked. (DALE, *seated* L., *opens her eyes and sits up. She looks around; suddenly realizes where she is and what is happening. She looks over her shoulder; sees open Hidden Room.* DALE *shudders; half rises.)*

DALE. Please close that awful door. I don't want to see it again. (DETECTIVE *goes up; closes the iron doors to Hidden Room.)*

BROOKS. *(Gets down on his knees beside* DALE*)* What happened to you? Can you remember?

DALE. I was here alone in the dark—then that door opened—*(Indicates door* R.*)*—and I saw a man come in. I hid in there. *(Indicates Hidden Room.)* It was the only thing I could think of.

DETECTIVE. *(*C. *Facing* DALE*)* And then——

DALE. He came in too, and closed the door, and I think he heard me gasp, for he turned a flashlight on me and said, "If you make a sound I'll kill you!" That's all I remember.

DETECTIVE. *(Looks at* DOCTOR, *then looks at* DALE; *suspiciously)* Do you *know* who that man was?

DALE. No. (DETECTIVE *looks at* DOCTOR.*)*

CORNELIA. But I do—it was The Bat!

DETECTIVE. *(Turns on her rather sardonically)* Ha! Still harping back to The Bat!

CORNELIA. I have every reason to believe The Bat is in this house.

DETECTIVE. *(Jeeringly)* And that he took the Union Bank money out of that safe, I suppose? No, Miss Van Gorder! *(Turns; faces* DOCTOR*)* Ask the Doctor who took the Union Bank money out of that safe. Ask the Doctor who attacked *me* downstairs in the drawing room; knocked *me* senseless, and locked *me* in the billiard room! *(To* DOCTOR. *Pause. Walks down* R.*)* The next time you put handcuffs on a man, be sure to take the key out of

his vest pocket! *(An astounded pause, then* COR-
NELIA *speaks.)*

CORNELIA. *(*L.C.*)* Perhaps I am an obstinate old
woman, but the Doctor and all the rest of us were
locked in the drawing room not ten minutes ago.

DETECTIVE. *(Sneeringly)* By The Bat, I suppose!

CORNELIA. *(Obstinately)* By the Bat! (DETEC-
TIVE *looks at* DOCTOR.) He went to the trouble to
leave his visiting card fastened to the door!

DETECTIVE. The Bat, eh? *(Confronts the* Doc-
TOR*)* You knew about this room, Wells?

DOCTOR. *(*R.C. *Looking up at* DETECTIVE*)* Yes.

DETECTIVE. And you knew the money was in the
room?

DOCTOR. Well, I was wrong, wasn't I?

DETECTIVE. You were up in this room, earlier tonight.

DOCTOR. No. I couldn't *get* up.

DETECTIVE. You know where that money is,
Wells, and I'm going to find out!

DOCTOR. *(Goaded beyond endurance)* Good God!
Do you suppose if I knew where it is I'd be here?
I've had plenty of chances to get away. No, you
can't pin anything on me, Anderson. It isn't criminal to have known that room is here.

DETECTIVE. Don't be so damned virtuous. Maybe
you haven't been upstairs. but unless I miss my
guess, you know who was. (DOCTOR's *face changes.
Crosses to* DOCTOR*)* What about Richard Fleming?

DOCTOR. *(Impressively)* I never killed him! I
don't even own a revolver!

DETECTIVE. *(Crosses down stage and front of*
DOCTOR *to* R. *As he goes)* You come with me, Wells.
This time I'll do the locking up. (DETECTIVE *stands
above door* R.; *looks at* CORNELIA. *As he takes
lighted candle off trunk as he crosses* R.*)* Better get

the young lady down to bed. I think that I can promise you a quiet night, from now on.

CORNELIA. *(Sardonically. To C.)* I'm glad you think so, Mr. Anderson! (DOCTOR *crosses past* DE-TECTIVE *; exits* R. DETECTIVE *follows* DOCTOR R.

(ELECTRICIAN catch movement of candle. Down to I candle. CORNELIA swiftly crosses over to door R.; closes it. Then she turns and faces DALE and BROOKS.)

DALE. *(L. with force)* I can't believe the Doctor killed Richard Fleming. (CORNELIA *crosses back to* C. *with lighted candle.* ELECTRICIAN *follow movement of candle.)*

CORNELIA. *(Swiftly moves to C.)* Of course he didn't. He's just guilty enough to look more guilty than he is. *(She moves up C. a little. Stands for a moment, then says to DALE)* But the man who was shut in the mantel room with you was the man who *killed* Richard Fleming, and took the money. (BROOKS *moves step out to L.C.)* But what brought him back? *(Pause. She looks at door R., then down at floor)* It's clear as a pikestaff. In some way he heard me coming—got out on the roof—*(Points L.)* —through the skylight—*(Points R.)*—and back here aga.. . *(To verify her theory about the roof, she goes up to window L.; looks out.* BROOKS *follows and stands up C., watching her. She then faces into room again; stands looking around, up C.)* But what brought him back? (BROOKS *crosses over L. Pause, while CORNELIA, candle in hand, moves quickly, now stooping to examine floor. Now straightens, looks about her. She also makes a careful search of the Hidden Room.* ELECTRICIAN *follows move-ment. Dims away down in foots when CORNELIA goes up into Hidden Room with candle. Catch light as CORNELIA comes out of Hidden Room. As she comes out of Hidden Room she partly closes the two iron doors.)*

BROOKS. *(Over L., watching her, as she comes down C.)* Is this something else you saw Mr. Gillette do?

CORNELIA. *(Over to R.C., at hamper)* I'm using my wits! I never saw *any* man do that. *(At last, with an air of great satisfaction, she sets candle on hamper R.C. Evidently she has made some important discovery)* I know very little about bank currency. Could such a sum be carried away in a man's pocket?

BROOKS. *(L.C.)* Even in bills of large denomination it would make a pretty sizable bundle.

(Enter LIZZIE R. with tumbler of wine in one hand and a lighted candle in the other. ELECTRICIAN catch light on her entrance. Follow her. This makes 2 candle light in foots. CORNELIA pursues her search of the room up R.C.)

LIZZIE. *(R., front of hamper)* That Jap broke the whiskey, but here's some of that elderberry wine. It's kind of comforting. Say, that assault and battery case is wandering all over the second floor. Think he's out of his head. I ran into him in the dark. I thought all my goose-flesh was standing on end before, but I raised a whole new crop. *(She goes back to door; kicks it shut with her foot. She crosses to C. CORNELIA crosses with candle to front of hamper. ELECTRICIAN follow movement of the two candles. LIZZIE towards DALE, who is seated L.)* I think there's a whole gang of crooks in this house. That Beresford—the Jap—and that assault and battery case—— Everybody pretending to be somebody he isn't! *(Starts)* Oh! *(She offers the wine to DALE, who shakes her head in refusal.)*

BROOKS. *(Down to* DALE, L.I, *with his arm about her)* Take it, Sweetheart.

LIZZIE. *(Stares, astounded; looks over at* COR-NELIA, R.C.*)* The gardener's calling her "Sweetheart."

CORNELIA. Oh, be still! He's *not* a gardener.

LIZZIE. My God! Another one! *(Then she raises wine to her lips; drinks it.* CORNELIA, *with the lighted candle, is working over* R., *below hamper, looking around room. As she gets near door* R. *she hears something. She makes gesture to others.* BERESFORD *gets cue through sight-hole in door. The* OTHERS *stand and watch. The door is suddenly thrown open and* BERESFORD *stands in the doorway, crouching, ready to spring. Sees them. His attitude relaxes. He looks rather sheepish.)*

BERESFORD. *(Smiles—in doorway)* Oh—it's you?

CORNELIA. *(*R.C.; *suspiciously)* Who did you *think* it was?

BERESFORD. *(Relieved)* I've been making a rather hectic search for the man who locked us in. But I didn't find a sign. *(He shuts the door. His eyes travel to* BROOKS. *He crosses over to* C. *In ugly tone)* Oh, still at large, Bailey?

BROOKS. *(Up close to him,* L.C.*)* I am, but the Doctor is not. Now, see here, Beresford, the situation has changed in the last few minutes—— (COR-NELIA, R.C., *puts candle on hamper.)* Doctor Wells is under arrest! I didn't mind your recognition of me—that was your duty—but I do object to the implication in your tone that I am a criminal. You've done your damndest—now cut it. (BILLY, *off* R., *turns DOORKNOB.* CORNELIA *lifts up candle.)*

CORNELIA. *(Faces door)* That doorknob's moving. (ALL *turn and look at door.)*

BERESFORD. *(In whisper to* CORNELIA*)* I'll open it. *(He crosses front of* CORNELIA *to door. Jerks* *open door.* BILLY, *who has hold of the off-stage side of doorknob, is jerked into room. Pause.)*

BILLY. *(Evidently very nervous, turns, steps back to door; looks off, then turns, faces others in room)* I come in, please? I not like to stay in dark.

CORNELIA. *(R.C.)* Come in. What is it, Billy? *(Steps forward a step or two.)*

BILLY. *(Nervously)* Man with sore head.

CORNELIA. What about him?

BILLY. Act very strange.

BERESFORD. *(Near door R.)* The man who fell into the room, downstairs?

BILLY. Yes—on second floor, walking around.

BERESFORD. *(To CORNELIA)* I was watching that fellow downstairs that fell in the room. I didn't think he was as dazed as he pretended to be.

CORNELIA. *(To BILLY, brightly)* Bring him up, Billy. (BILLY *starts to go, then turn back; faces* CORNELIA.)

BILLY. *(Nervously—over to CORNELIA, R.C.)* You give candle, please? Don't like dark.

CORNELIA. *(Hands lighted candle to trembling* BILLY*)* Billy, what did you see when you came running down the stairs, before we were locked in?

BILLY. *(Candle shakes in his hand, nervously)* Nothing! (BROOKS *now stands* C., *between* CORNELIA *and* LIZZIE.)

LIZZIE. *(L.C. Feeling the wine somewhat)* It must have been some nothing to make him drop a bottle of whiskey.

BILLY. Ghost walk in house! *(Backs away towards door R.)*

LIZZIE. *(Leaning close to* BROOKS, *shivering)* Ghosts! It makes my very switch stand on end! *(She puts the bottom of the glass on the flame of candle. ELECTRICIAN catches this. Candle out. Almost at same time* BILLY *disappears off door* R. *with lighted candle. Stage dark.)*

BERESFORD. Can't we have a light?
BROOKS. Wait, I'll——

(STAGE MANAGER with whip does BAT EFFECT. Strange flapping sound is heard, first in one part of the room and then the other. Hits back of scene near ceiling on cues.)

CORNELIA. *(Sharply, after a moment)* What's that?
LIZZIE. *(L.C. Plaintively)* If you hear anything, it's my teeth chattering.
CORNELIA. Take them out and put them in your pocket. *(BAT EFFECT again.)*
BERESFORD. *(After a moment)* That's odd! There *is* something moving around the room. *(BAT EFFECT again.)*
BROOKS. *(C.)* It's up near the ceiling.
LIZZIE. *(Slow wail)* Oh—h—h—— *(BAT EFFECT again.)*
BERESFORD. Good God! It hit me in the face. *(He slaps hands together.)*
LIZZIE. I'm going! I don't know where, but I'm going. *(She quickly crosses R. and up above hamper. BAT EFFECT again. She screams)* It's in my hair! It's in my hair!
BROOKS. *(Voice in the dark, crosses R., then back to L.)* I've got it! It's a Bat! *(Scream from LIZZIE. He goes up quickly to window L.; throws something out. There is a pause.)*
CORNELIA. *(Down L.C., facing up stage)* Lizzie— *(Pause)* Lizzie, where are you?
LIZZIE. *(On her knees back of hamper up R.— voice out of the gloom)* Trying to crawl under the floor. I'd go down a rathole if there was one. *(Door R. slowly opens and BILLY, leading the UNKNOWN MAN, enters. BILLY upstage side, UNKNOWN down stage side. BILLY leads him to C. ELECTRICIAN*

catch candle BILLY *carries. Follow movement to* C.
LIZZIE *gets rid of her glass and dead candle as she
kneels behind hamper. She places them on floor behind hamper.)*

BERESFORD. Come in. *(Steps to* R.C. *end of hamper; gets the chair without back; places it well down*
C.) Sit down. (BERESFORD *steps back and stands
above* UNKNOWN C.)

CORNELIA. (L.C. *To* UNKNOWN, *who sits down)*
Are you better now?

UNKNOWN. *(Slowly)* Somewhat.

CORNELIA. Lizzie, give him some wine.

LIZZIE. *(Back of hamper* R.C., *head just in sight)*
Somebody drank it.

CORNELIA. *(Speaks to* BILLY) Billy, you can go.

BILLY. *(Who is* R.C., *turns, goes a few steps* R.,
then turns back to CORNELIA. *His tone is fairly
pitiful)* I stay, please.

BROOKS. *(L. of* CORNELIA. *Watches* BILLY *suspiciously, then to* CORNELIA) Anderson intimated
that the Doctor had an accomplice in the house.
(Crosses to R.C. *and* BILLY, *front of the other characters.* BROOKS *close up to* BILLY, *on his* L.) Why
isn't this the man? *(Takes the candle from* BILLY.)

BILLY. (R.C. *Cringing)* Please, no.

BROOKS. *(Puts candle on hamper, catches* BILLY
*by the shoulders and half turns him to look up at
the Hidden Room, up stage* C.) Did you know that
room was there?

BILLY. No.

CORNELIA. He couldn't have locked us in. He
was *with* us.

BROOKS. He may *know* who did it. *(To* BILLY)
Do you? (BILLY *shivers.)* Who did you see at the
head of the small staircase? *(*BROOKS *swings* BILLY
in half circle around R.) Now we're through with
nonsense. I want the truth.

BILLY. See face. That's all.

BROOKS. *(Strong)* *Whose* face?

BILLY. *(Evidently lying)* Don't know. *(Looks down.)*

· CORNELIA. Never mind Billy—*(Looks at* UN-KNOWN MAN*)* Solve the mystery of *this* man and we may get at the facts. (BERESFORD *holds lighted candle up* C. *above* UNKNOWN. BROOKS *has turned when* CORNELIA *speaks. Takes eyes off* BILLY, *who has started on tiptoes for door* R. *Just as he gets to door,* BROOKS *turns and sees* BILLY *trying to get away.)*

BROOKS. *(Takes a step or two toward* BILLY*)* You stay here. (BILLY *stops; stands below door* R.)

BERESFORD. This chap—*(Indicating* UNKNOWN*)* —claims to have lost his memory. I suppose a blow on the head might do that. I don't know.

LIZZIE. *(Back of hamper* R.C.*)* I wish somebody would knock *me* on the head. *I'd* like to forget a few things.

CORNELIA. *(To* UNKNOWN*)* Don't you remember even your name?

UNKNOWN. *(Shakes head)* Not—yet.

CORNELIA. Or where you came from? (UN-KNOWN *shakes his head.)* Do you remember how you got into this house?

UNKNOWN. *(With difficulty)* Yes, I remember that, all right. *(He puts hand to his head)* My head aches—to beat the band.

CORNELIA. How did you happen to come to this house?

UNKNOWN. *(Slowly)* Saw the lights.

BROOKS. *(*R.C. *quickly)* Where were you when you saw the lights?

UNKNOWN. I broke out of the garage.

BERESFORD. *(Up* C.*)* How did you get there?

UNKNOWN. I don't know.

BROOKS. *(With keen suspicion)* Had you been robbed?

UNKNOWN. Everything gone—out of my pockets.

BROOKS. *(Stepping closer to* UNKNOWN*)* Including your watch?

UNKNOWN. If I had a watch, it's gone. All my papers—are—gone.

CORNELIA. *(Suspiciously)* How do *you* know you *had* papers?

UNKNOWN. *(Looks front; haltingly)* Most men —carry papers, don't they? I'm dazed, but my mind's all right. If you ask me—I think I'm d-d-damned funny. (BROOKS *and* BERESFORD *exchange glances.)*

CORNELIA. (L.C.) Did you ring the house phone? (BROOKS *and* BERESFORD *change places.)*

UNKNOWN. Yes. *(A start from* CORNELIA *and* BROOKS*)* I leaned against the button in the garage —then, I think maybe I fainted. That's not clear. (DALE *rises.)*

DALE. *(Leaning over, and looking at* UNKNOWN; *brightly)* You don't remember how you were hurt?

UNKNOWN. No. The first thing I remember I was in the garage, tied. I was gagged, too—that's what's the matter with my tongue now. Then I got myself free--and got out of a window.

BERESFORD. Just a moment, Miss Van Gorder— Anderson ought to be here for this. *(On word "Anderson,"* DALE *sits again* L.)

(ELECTRICIAN follow movement of candle. BERESFORD *starts for door* R. *He gets to* R.C. *When* DETECTIVE *enters,* R., *he closes the door after him. On word "Anderson,"* UNKNOWN'S *face shows intense alertness. THE UNKNOWN gets to his feet. DETECTIVE has closed the door before he catches sight of the* UNKNOWN. *He stands rigid, his hand still on the knob of the*

door. It is to be remembered the DETECTIVE
has not yet seen or heard of the UNKNOWN.*)*

CORNELIA. *(Raises voice, watching* ANDERSON*)*
A new element in our mystery, Mr. Anderson.
(Slight pause. DETECTIVE *and* UNKNOWN *look at
each other for a moment. The* UNKNOWN'S *face is
a blank and expressionless.)* Quite dazed, poor fellow! (UNKNOWN *sways.)*

DETECTIVE. *(Slowly)* How did *he* get into the
house?

CORNELIA. He came through the terrace door
some time ago, just before we were locked in.

DETECTIVE. *(Dryly)* Doesn't remember anything,
eh? *(Crosses to* R.C. *to* UNKNOWN. BERESFORD
crosses over same time with candle; stands up C.
DETECTIVE *speaks roughly and puts hand under* UN-
KNOWN'S *chin; jerks* UNKNOWN'S *head up)* Look
up here! (UNKNOWN *looks up at* DETECTIVE *with a
blank face.)* Look up, you—— *(Same business.)*
This losing your memory stuff doesn't go down
with me!

UNKNOWN. *(Weakly)* It doesn't go down very
well with me, either!

DETECTIVE. Did you ever see me before? (BERES-
FORD *holds the candle a little nearer* DETECTIVE'S
face.)

UNKNOWN. *(Looks at* DETECTIVE; *slight pause,
haltingly)* You're the Doctor I saw downstairs,
aren't you?

DETECTIVE. *(Takes the watch of Act II from his
pocket; holds it out towards* UNKNOWN*)* Does this
watch belong to you? *(Looks suspiciously at* UN-
KNOWN.*)*

UNKNOWN. *(Looks at watch)* Maybe—— *(Falls
back against* BROOKS*)* I don't know.

CORNELIA. *(L.C.)* He has evidently been attacked.

He claims to have recovered consciousness in the garage, where he was tied, hand and foot.

DETECTIVE. He does, eh? If you'll give me five minutes alone with him, I'll get the *truth* out of him!

CORNELIA. *(Half turning back to* DETECTIVE*)* Do you believe that money is irrevocably gone?

DETECTIVE. There's no such word as "irrevocable" in my vocabulary, but I believe it's out of the house, if that's what you mean.

CORNELIA. Suppose I tell you that there are certain facts that you have overlooked?

DETECTIVE. *(Sardonically, to* CORNELIA, *but looks at* UNKNOWN*)* Still on the trail!

CORNELIA. I was right about the Doctor, wasn't I? *(Goes to door* R.*)*

DETECTIVE. Just fifty percent right, and the Doctor didn't turn the trick alone. Now, if you'll all go out and close that door—— *(*CORNELIA *looks off* R. *Takes candle from* BROOKS.*)*

CORNELIA. *(Starts out* R.*)* Quick! A man just went through that skylight and out onto the roof.

DETECTIVE. Out onto the roof!

BROOKS. Come on, Beresford!

(LIGHTS OUT when CORNELIA *exits* R. CORNELIA *exits.* BROOKS *(2),* DETECTIVE *(3),* BERESFORD *(4),* BILLY *(5), and closes door behind him. Ad lib. from the* MEN *as they run off* R., *"A man on the roof," etc. Talking and excitement and noise of running. As the* DETECTIVE *goes off* R. *he draws his revolver.)*

BERESFORD. Righto—— *(*DALE, LIZZIE *and* UNKNOWN *remain in room. In the dark, except for the light from doorway* R.*)*

LIZZIE. *(Goes over to* DALE L.C.*)* I'd **run** if my legs would!

DALE. Hush!

LIZZIE. *(Wails)* How do we know *this fellow right here* isn't *The Bat? (Indicating the* UN-KNOWN, *who has half risen, back into chair.* COR-NELIA *re-enters with lighted candle.* ELECTRI-CIAN *catch candle* R. CORNELIA *comes in very cautiously, looks over her shoulder, and quietly closes the door.)*

DALE. What did you see?

CORNELIA. *(Calmly)* I didn't see anything! I had to get rid of that dratted detective before I assassinated him. *(She crosses to* L.C.*)*

DALE. Nobody went through the skylight?

CORNELIA. *(Few steps to* R.C.*)* They have now—the whole outfit. *(Up a step* L.C.*)*

DALE. Then why did you——

CORNELIA. *(Interrupting)* Because that money's in this room. If the man who took it out of the safe had got away with it, why did he come back and hide there? *(Indicates Hidden Room. They look up at Hidden Room.)* He got it out of the safe, and that's as far as he *did* get it! There's a *hat* behind that safe—a man's soft felt hat.

LIZZIE. *(Up* L.*)* Oh, I wish he'd take his hat and go home. *(*UNKNOWN *listens intently.)*

CORNELIA. *(Disregarding* LIZZIE; *goes over* R.C., *up stage in front of the closets, back of the hamper. On floor she picks up a half-burned candle)* A half-burned candle. Another thing the detective overlooked. *(She steps back to* C.; *looks from candle to closet. Suddenly at the window* BROOKS *quickly lowers himself in from the roof ladder on downstage side of window* L.*)*

LIZZIE. *(Horrified, runs down* L.C.*)* Oh, my God, another one! *(*CORNELIA *gets her revolver from top of hamper; points at the figure of* BROOKS.*)*

DALE. *(Recognizes* BROOKS; *puts her hand up so* CORNELIA *won't shoot)* It's Jack! *(*DALE *is now up*

L.C., *then over to* BROOKS *as he comes in window.*
CORNELIA, *on seeing that it is* BROOKS, *lays her revolver on top of hamper,* R.C. UNKNOWN *sees her do this.)*

BROOKS. *(Up at window* L.*)* The man Lizzie saw drop from the skylight probably reached the roof from this window—easiest thing in the world.

CORNELIA. *(*R.C. *upstage; looks at the closets* R.C.*)* Never mind the window! When that detective comes back I may have a *surprise party* for him! (DALE *crosses* C. *toward* CORNELIA *to* L.C.*)*

LIZZIE. *(*L.C.*)* No more surprises for me. I've been surprised pretty near to death all night.

DALE. *(Up* L. *to* BROOKS*)* Aunt Cornelia thinks the money's still here. (LIZZIE *sits, chair over* L.*)*

CORNELIA. *(Over to closet up* R.*; opens the three closets, up* R. *to* R.C.*)* I *know* it's here. (BROOKS *crosses to* CORNELIA, *crossing* DALE.*)*

(ELECTRICIAN follow movement of candle as
    CORNELIA *moves, opening and closing the closets.* BROOKS *crosses* R. *of* CORNELIA. LIZZIE
    sits still, her eyes rivetted on the UNKNOWN,
    who is looking over R. *at revolver on hamper.*
    DALE *looks at* LIZZIE, *then steps down* L. *to*
    LIZZIE.*)*

DALE. *(Nervously)* Lizzie—— What are you looking at?

*(*UNKNOWN *is again sunk in apathy.* CORNELIA *resumes trying of the closet doors. She is now at the closet that is* R.C. *that is placed up and down stage.)*

CORNELIA. This one is locked, and the key gone.
LIZZIE. *(Seated* L.*; crying)* If there's anything locked up in that closet, you'd better let it stay.

There's enough running around loose in this house as it is. *(There is no question about the interest in the* UNKNOWN'S *face.* BROOKS *up and stands back of* CORNELIA C. CORNELIA *hands* BROOKS *the candle.)*

CORNELIA. Lizzie, did you ever take that key?

LIZZIE. *(Seated* L.*)* No'm.

CORNELIA. It may be locked from the inside. (DALE *up beside* BROOKS; *watches* CORNELIA *at closet* R.C.*)* I'll soon find out. (CORNELIA *takes from her hair a wire hairpin and runs it through the keyhole.* There's no key inside. (BROOKS *shakes the door of closet but it does not yield.)* I want to see the inside of that closet.

LIZZIE. If you could see *my* insides, you wouldn't recognize them.

CORNELIA. Bring me the other closet keys. (DALE, *with the candle, goes to closet up* L.; *then down to closet* L. *below the window. Gets key.* LIZZIE *follows* DALE *and the candle.)*

(ELECTRICIAN follows the movement of the candle. DALE *up to* CORNELIA *and gives her key.* LIZZIE *follows her. Meanwhile* BROOKS *goes to closets against back wall,* R.C.; *gets keys. During above business,* UNKNOWN, *with infinite caution, moves his chair over* R. *toward revolver* CORNELIA *has left on top of hamper* R.C. *He reaches out, gets revolver, moves back chair to* C. *and sits same as before. After letting audience see revolver, he partly covers it.)*

CORNELIA. *(*C.*)* There! That unlocked it!

BROOKS. *(Up* R.C.*)* I'd keep *back* a little. You don't know *what* may be inside. (CORNELIA *and* DALE *draw back, stepping down and* L.*)*

LIZZIE. *(Shivering, speaks as she crosses front of* UNKNOWN, *over to front of hamper* R.C.*)* Mercy sakes, who *wants* to know! (LIZZIE *sits on the hamper.* BROOKS *takes the candle, and slowly and cautiously opens the door of the closet. He stands for a moment and stares, appalled at something on the floor of the closet.)*

(ELECTRICIAN dim away down while this business being done. BROOKS *looks into closet. ELECTRICIAN comes up on the foots when* BROOKS *closes closet. Pause.* BROOKS *comes down few steps* C.)*

DALE. *(Over* L.; *aghast)* What is it? What did you see? *(Staring at* BROOKS.)

BROOKS. *(Does not answer; then pulling himself together)* Miss Cornelia, I think we have found the ghost the Jap butler saw. How are your nerves?

CORNELIA. *(Holds out her hand)* Give me the candle. *(He does.* BROOKS *crosses over* L. *to* DALE. *They stand and watch* CORNELIA.)

(ELECTRICIAN follow and dim in foots as CORNELIA *goes up and away down when she opens closet door. Come up again in foots when* CORNELIA *closes door of closet and comes down again.* UNKNOWN *half turns and watches the others out of the corner of his eye. After* CORNELIA *looks in closet she closes door of closet; turns; faces* BROOKS *and* DALE. *A tense pause.)*

CORNELIA. It is Courtleigh Fleming.

BROOKS. *(Up* L.C.) It *was* Courtleigh Fleming.

DALE. *(L. with hand on back of chair)* Then he did not die in the West.

BROOKS. *(Up* L.C.) He died in this house— within the last hour. The body is still warm, and Doctor Wells killed him.

CORNELIA. *(Comes down* L.C.*)* I wonder! *(Then*

to Brooks *as she crosses to* Dale, l.*)* Please look
and see if Courtleigh Fleming wore a wrist watch
with a luminous dial. (Brooks *up to closet; opens
down-stage door; gets on his knees; puts arm in
closet. Time for brief examination. Rises; closes
closet door; comes down* l.c.*)*

Brooks. Yes.

Cornelia. *(To* Dale*)* The *eye* Lizzie saw was
the wrist-watch. *(The* Unknown *sinks down in
chair, but listens intensely.)*

Brooks. Isn't it clear, Miss Van Gorder? The
Doctor and old Mr. Fleming formed a conspiracy—
Fleming to rob the bank and hide the money here.
Wells to issue a false death certificate in the West,
and bury a substitute body, secured God knows
how. It was easy—it kept clear the name of the
President of the Union Bank—and it put the blame
on me. *(Comes down* c. *Turns quickly and looks
up at* Cornelia*)* Only they slipped up in one place.
Dick Fleming leased the house to you, and they
couldn't get it back.

Cornelia. *(Quickly)* Then you think that to·
night Courtleigh Fleming broke in, with the Doc·
tor's assistance, and that he killed Dick, his own
nephew, from the staircase?

Brooks. Don't you?

Cornelia. No.

Brooks. *(Up a step, facing* Cornelia*)* It's as
clear as crystal. Wells tried to get out of the house
tonight with that blueprint. *Why?* He knew the
minute we got it we'd come up here, and Fleming
was here.

Cornelia. Perfectly true, and then?

Brooks. Old Fleming killed Dick, and Wells
killed Fleming. *(Crossing over to* l. *to* Dale, *below her, downstage) You can't get away from it!*

Cornelia. No—no, the Doctor is not a murderer.
He's as puzzled as we are about some things. **He**

and Courtleigh Fleming were working together, but remember this—Doctor Wells was locked in the drawing room with us. He's been trying all evening to get up the stairs and failed.

BROOKS. *(Down L.)* He was here ten minutes ago, locked in this room.

CORNELIA. I grant you that—but at the same time an unknown masked man was locked in that mantel room with Dale. The Doctor put out the candle when you opened that hidden room. *Why?* Because *he thought Courtleigh Fleming was hiding there.* But at this moment he believes that Fleming has made his escape. No—we haven't solved the mystery yet—— There's another element—an *unknown* element—and that element is—the *Bat!*

DALE. *(As she crosses quickly to R. downstage, front of* UNKNOWN *and well over to R. Half hysterically)* Oh, call the detective. Let's get through with this thing. I can't *bear* any more.

CORNELIA. Wait. Not yet. Nobody can help Courtleigh Fleming, and I'm not through. *(Goes well up C.)*

LIZZIE. *(Seated on hamper R.C.)* Well, I'm through, all right!

CORNELIA. *(Over to R.C.; looks and sees hamper)* Open the lid of that hamper. *(Indicates hamper which* LIZZIE *is sitting on)* And see what's inside. *(BROOKS crosses over to R.C., back of hamper; opens lid; looks inside.)*

BROOKS. Nothing here but some clothes and books.

CORNELIA. *(L. of BROOKS)* Books? I left no books in that hamper.

BROOKS. *(Reading title of cheap paper novel)* "Little Rosebud's Lovers, or a Cruel Revenge," by Laura Jean——

LIZZIE. *(Down below hamper R.)* That's mine! Oh, Miss Neillie, I tell you this house is haunted. I left that book in my satchel, along with "Wedded But No Wife" and—— (BROOKS *closes lid of hamper.)*

CORNELIA. *(Up* C.) Where's your satchel?

LIZZIE *(Looks around front of hamper and leans over hamper; looks behind it and around on the floor* R. *of hamper)* Where's my satchel? My satchel—— My satchel's gone. *(Over hamper at end.* CORNELIA *holds candle high. Gets candle from* BROOKS; *goes* L. *ELECTRICIAN follows movement of candle.)*

CORNELIA. *(At last sees satchel, above window* L.2, *on floor, where* MASKED MAN *left it when he darted into the Hidden Room earlier in Act. Indicating it)* Isn't that your satchel, Lizzie? (LIZZIE *quickly over to* CORNELIA, *then crosses to above window; looks scared; then looks at* CORNELIA.)

LIZZIE. Yes, ma'm.

CORNELIA. *(Points to chair down* L.) Put it there. (LIZZIE *stalls, scared.* CORNELIA *continues to point at chair.)*

LIZZIE. I'm scared to touch it. It may have a bomb in it! *(She reluctantly gets the satchel; carries it very slowly between thumb and forefinger as she might carry a loaded gun.)*

CORNELIA. Do as I tell you—put it on that chair. (LIZZIE *deposits the satchel on chair down* L. *and backs away up* L., *near window.* CORNELIA *starting over* C., *up stage, looking at* BROOKS *and* DALE. DALE *over* R., *behind hamper.* BROOKS R. *of her. To* BROOKS) You open it. If the money's there, you're the one who ought to find it.

(BROOKS *looks at* DALE, *then with a smile crosses front of* CORNELIA. DALE *follows him.* CORNELIA, *with candle, follows them to* L.C. BROOKS *fumbles at catch of satchel on chair down* L., DALE *beside him. While they are occupied with*

this business, UNKNOWN *rises and quickly gets
to door* R.; *faces the others, his back to door.
With hand behind him, he locks the door, takes
the key out, and puts it in his pocket. Meanwhile* BROOKS *has succeeded in opening the
satchel.* BROOKS *and* DALE *show they are de-
lighted as they see the canvas bag with the
packages of money in it.)*

BROOKS. The money is here.
DALE. Oh, thank God!

*(ELECTRICIAN—During above red glow starts
faintly outside window, increases and goes up
and down. Flame effect. Crackling of burning
wood heard off* L. ALL *stand; watch window
as red glare fills room.)*

LIZZIE. Fire!
BERESFORD. *(Off* R.*)* The garage is burning!

*(Sound of men's VOICES and RUNNING of feet
on tin, supposed to be the roof.* CORNELIA,
BROOKS, DALE *and* LIZZIE *all turn towards door*
R. *Suddenly their attention is rivetted on the*
UNKNOWN, *who is standing in front of door* R.
*His back to door, facing the other characters, he
has the revolver in his hand.)*

UNKNOWN. *(Savage tone)* This door is locked
and the key is in my pocket—— (LIZZIE *opens her
mouth to scream. He looks at her and in an ominous tone)* Not a sound out of *you. (To* BROOKS*)*
Close that bag—*(Referring to satchel)*—and put it
back where you found it.
BROOKS. *(Starts toward him a step) You!*
DALE. *(Up* C.*)* Jack!
CORNELIA. *(*R.C. *to* BROOKS*)* Do what he tells

you! (BROOKS *closes bag, and puts it up above win-dow* L.)

LIZZIE. *(Horrified whisper,* R. *of* DALE*)* It's the Bat!

UNKNOWN. *(At door* R.*)* Blow out that candle! (CORNELIA, *after a moment's hesitation, blows out candle. LIGHTS OUT. Only LIGHT in room now is the flicker from fire outside window* L.*)*

LIZZIE. *(Hysterically)* I'm going to scream! I can't keep it back.

UNKNOWN. *(Over* R. *at door; savagely)* Put that woman in that mantel room—*(Points up* C.*)*—and shut her up. (BROOKS *pushes* LIZZIE *up to mantel.)*

LIZZIE. *(As she goes up* C.*)* Don't shove! I'm damn glad to go. *(She goes in Hidden Room.* BROOKS *closes the iron doors behind her.)*

UNKNOWN. *(Unlocks the* R. *door; opens it a little; listens; closes it without locking it)* Not a sound, if you value your lives. *(Crosses over to* L.C., *up stage)* In a moment or two a man will come into this room, either through the door or by that window. *(Step toward window; then back to* C.*)* The man who started the fire to draw you out of this house.

BROOKS. *(Up* L.C. *one step toward* UNKNOWN*)* For God's sake don't keep these women here!

UNKNOWN. Keep them here where we can watch them! Don't you understand? There's a *killer* loose!

(ELECTRICIAN—The red glow dies out. Only the blue light outside window now. UNKNOWN *steps down* L.*)*

CORNELIA. *(Up* C.; *to* UNKNOWN*)* I have understood very clearly for the last hour. The man who struck you down and tied you in the garage, the man who killed Dick Fleming and stabbed that poor wretch in the closet, the man who locked us in downstairs, and removed the money from the safe—the man who started that fire outside is——

UNKNOWN. (*As if hearing some one outside window, puts up his hand*) Sh! (*He runs quickly over to door* R., *locks it, and hurries back to* C., *up stage*) Stand back out of the light. The ladder!

(DALE *and* CORNELIA *stand back* R.C. BROOKS *up stage above window* L. UNKNOWN *flattens his body against wall up* L. *beside* BROOKS. *The ladder is seen to shake, outside the window. A breathless pause, then outside on the ladder* THE BAT *is faintly outlined coming up ladder, in cap and black silk handkerchief disguise. He steps in window, and backs up to get the grip. As he does this,* UNKNOWN *and* BROOKS *grab him, just as* BAT *focusses flashlight on the satchel. There is a struggle in the dark.* BROOKS *and* UNKNOWN *overpower* THE BAT.)

UNKNOWN. (*To* BROOKS) Get his gun. (*Pause*) Got it?

BROOKS. Yes.

UNKNOWN. (*Up above* THE BAT, BROOKS *below* THE BAT) Hold out your hands, Bat, while I put on the bracelets! (*Puts handcuffs on* BAT'S *wrists*) Sometimes even the *cleverest* Bat comes through a window at night and is caught! Double murder—burglary, and arson—— That's a good night's work even for you, Bat! (UNKNOWN *turns flashlight on* THE BAT's *face*) Take off that hankerchief. (BROOKS *does this business, revealing* ANDERSON, *the detective.* UNKNOWN *above* ANDERSON, BROOKS *below him.* DETECTIVE *is covered with two revolvers. The storm being over, the LIGHTS flash on. ELECTRICIAN—Four strips in foots come up full.*)

DALE. *(Up* R.C. *with* CORNELIA*)* It's Mr. Anderson!

UNKNOWN. *(Without taking his eyes off* THE BAT*)* I'm Anderson. This man has been impersonating me. You're a good actor, Bat, for a fellow that's such a *bad* actor! How did you get your dope on this case? Did you tap the wires to Headquarters?

(WARN Curtain.)

THE BAT. *(With sardonic smile)* I'll tell you that when I—— *(With swift movement, though handcuffed, he jerks the revolver by the barrel from the real* ANDERSON, *wheels on* BROOKS *with lightning rapidity, brings down the butt of revolver on* BROOKS' *wrist.* BROOKS' *revolver drops to floor.* THE BAT *swings to* R.C., *keeping the characters covered with gun. Speaks as he moves or backs away to* R.C.*)* Hands up, everybody! (CORNELIA *has not raised her hands.)* Hands up—you! *(Savagely to* CORNELIA.*)*

CORNELIA. *(Coming down* C.*)* Why, I took the bullets out of that revolver two hours ago. (THE BAT *throws the revolver toward her. It drops in front of her on floor. As soon as* THE BAT *drops revolver, the* UNKNOWN *picks up the other gun, and runs back of* CORNELIA *and blocks* THE BAT'S *getaway* R.C. UNKNOWN *covers* BAT *with gun.)*

UNKNOWN. *(To* BAT*)* Don't move! (CORNELIA *picks up her gun from the floor.)* You see, you never know what a woman will do! *(Tauntingly to* BAT, *who turns* R. *and growls at* UNKNOWN.*)*

CORNELIA. *(Breaks the revolver and the loaded shells fall to floor.* THE BAT *wheels and looks at her, and bullets on floor.)* As it happened, I didn't. The first lie of an otherwise stainless life!

CURTAIN FALLS

On SECOND CURTAIN, LIZZIE *sticks her head out of Hidden Room, scared, and disappears into Hidden Room again.*

THE END

"THE BAT"

PROPERTY PLOT

ACTS I AND II

1 Library table.
5 Single chairs.
1 Armchair.
3 Small stands (two for lamps, one for telephone up R.)
1 Console (or half table).
1 Tall pedestal with basket of spring flowers.
1 Settee, 4 sofa pillows. Cretonne covers for furniture and pillows.
Fireplace furniture.
Fire screen.
1 Large rug.
Ground cloth or carpet.
Carpet on stairs.
1 Mantel clock.
6 Cream-colored shades on French window.
Bag golf-sticks.
2 Telephones.
Ouija board and prayer book up Center.
Evening paper on settee L.C.
Piece of broken glass on floor front of window, L.C.
Roll of three blueprints (15 inches by 3) in bookcase top shelf. up Left, above fireplace, hidden behind books.
Small piece of blueprint on floor inside fire fender L.
Reading-glass on Center library table.

Box of matches in holder, library table.

2 Door-keys with tags attached, on library table.

Cloth-covered book on library table.

Small revolver in table drawer (with fake bullets). These bullets important—must work easy and fall out when gun is broken open Act III.

Dozen real books in top shelf of wall bookcase, L. above fireplace.

Prop. books in other shelves, and in wall bookcase down R.1, up R.3 and up Center.

Door-keys in doors and L.3.

Bolt on terrace door up R.3 in alcove (Carpenter).

Also strong cord at bottom of terrace door, off stage, to work

Cue near end of Act II. (Door is open. Cue to close it given.)

Pane of glass set in one of the frames of French window doors. (To break from outside on cue.)

Small hammer and flat stone with Note tied to stone, placed outside of French windows, to be thrown into room through broken window, on cue.

Small props off R. on two prop tables.:

Six cheap tin candle-sticks and candles, 4 boxes of parlor matches, box of matches for Dale.

Flashlights (pocket-size) for Doctor (see Elec. Plot), for Beresford, for Detective, for Unknown Man, for Brooks (in case one Cornelia carries end of Act II goes out).

1 Small and 1 large flash for Detective.

2 Illuminated wrist watches. (Small electric light, covered and placed in leather wrist watch holders—One for Beresford and one for Stage Manager.)

Doctor's black bag—containing key-ring and keys, piece of blueprint, paper powder box.

1 Revolver for Beresford.

2 Sure-fire revolvers for stage manager.

1 Revolver for Detective and pair of handcuffs.
Key-ring and keys for Richard Fleming.
Photograph of Brooks.
Coffee pot, half filled with burnt sugar and water.
White napkin for Lizzie.
Round silver tray with common white plate, cup and saucer.
Prop Parker House roll and prop chop—for Lizzie.
Thunder drum, placed well up stage off R.
Wind machine, placed well up stage off R.
Long bamboo stick with padded wooden hammer, attached to end, for effect—noise up stage (supposed to be noise of hammering upstairs).
Electric bell (doorbell off R.2.).
Third Act, solid door braced and set well off stage R.2 for slam.
Water bottle (filled with sand) off R. for Lizzie.
Large butcher knife off R. for Billy and Lizzie—double on it.
Tray, two water-glasses and small water-pitcher with water, off R.2.
Valance—11 feet seven inches long, over French window, 18 inches deep.
Cretonne, same material used on furniture.
Doors of window must open in and on stage.

ACT II—SAME SET AS ACT I

Discovered: On floor prop Parker House roll. (Made to open. Dale hides blueprint in this.) Front of table c.
Off on stairs, R.3: Prop raincoat for Dale, pair of ladies' rubbers.
Envelopes for Brooks, half covered with ink, supposed to be soot.
Black cardboard Bat, with thumb tacks, for Property Man to place on right-hand double door

up R.3, leading to alcove, on cue near end of Act II.

Large white handkerchief for Doctor. Used as a gag for Detective.

Rubber base telephone. Placed instead of real phone used in Act I. Up Center.

Small tray of broken glass for glass crash off R.3.

Straw hat for Beresford.

Writing paper and lead pencil up stage C.

Bag and knitting for Cornelia (furnished by character).

Cigarette case and cigarettes for Doctor.

Cigarette case and cigarettes for Beresford.

Cigarette case and cigarettes for Fleming.

Detective badge for Detective.

Old silver watch for Beresford.

Armful of wood for Brooks.

Cigar for Detective.

ACT III

Ground cloth.

1 Kitchen chair with back.

1 Kitchen chair without back.

2 Old-fashioned small trunks, 1 large hamper.

6 Old wooden boxes (size soap boxes).

Old-fashioned sewing-machine.

2 Old second-hand dress-suit cases.

Dozen paper boxes (shoe boxes).

2 Paper hat boxes.

3 Bundles, wrapped in brown paper, on shelf of closets up R. and R.C.

Men and women's old clothes in hamper.

Black handkerchiefs (two) for Detective.

Pair of rubbers for Detective.

Lighted candle discovered front of prop safe up C. in Hidden Room.

White canvas bag, 18 by 10 inches, with draw

string. Paper money in bundle in bag. Discovered in safe.

Sir closet keys. Discovered in six of the seven closets in room.

Closet up R.C., facing Left, has no key.

Key in door R.2 (on stage side).

Act II revolver (with the fake bullets) for Cornelia—off R.2.

Matches on top trunk R.C. (Discovered.)

Lady's old black satchel—contains 2 old shirt waists, 2 cheap paper-backed novels.

Extension ladder placed outside window up L.3 out of sight at rise. Placed in trap outside window. To come up on cue given. (Carpenter dept.)

Ladder placed below window (down stage). Effect of climbing to roof. (Carpenter dept.)

Half dozen candles and candle holders off R. Matches.

Tumbler of grape juice off R. for Lizzie.

Piece of sheet iron (roofing tin), six feet long by four. For effect of running on the roof.

Crate (wooden box) to break. Effect of breaking through a door. Off R.

Crackling fire effect—burning wood—off L.

Handcuffs of Act II double this Act (Unknown Man used them).

Horsewhip, off R., for Stage Manager (for Bat effect).

Small rug up in Hidden Room on floor, Left, in front of sofa.

Small piece of half-burned candle on floor back of hamper R.C.

Rumble of thunder. Just before curtain rises. Lights full up. At rise.

See that double doors are open—up R.3.

Piece of glass on floor up L.C., front French windows.

Piece of blueprint in fender at fireplace.
Clock on mantel set at 10.30.
Window shades down.
See that small revolver with fake bullets is in table
    drawer, Center.

ELECTRIC PLOT

Use 4 Strips, 6 Lights to Strip, 60 Watt Lamps. In
    Foots, 1 Blue Lamp, 4 Amber, 1 Pink to a Strip.
In First Border.. 4.. 3..Light Section DELRAY
    100 W Nitrogen lamps.
In First Border:
No. 1 Sec. (R) 1 Pink Color—2 Amber Colors.
No. 2 Sec. (R) 2 Amber Color—1 Pink Color.
No. 3 Sec. (C) 1 Pink Color—2 Amber Colors.
No. 4 Sec. (L) 2 Amber Colors—1 Pink Colors.
Company Switch Board consists of 4 Cutler Ham-
    mer Interlocking Dimmers to control foots and
    first border.
Each section and border light connects together at
    Switch board.
To be controlled separately or together.
1 Dimmer Control Brackets on set (Act I and II).
1 Dimmer for Fireplace Lamp and Log L.2 (Act I
    and II) and Fire Box and Spot Lamps off L.3
    (window Act III).
2 Dimmers control blue lamps Act III.
Chandelier, Act III, Switch on company box.
Act I—At Rise—Foots and borders full up.
    Bracket Lamps—2 to a bracket—
        Placed on wall below door R.2.
        Placed on wall above door R.2.
        Placed on wall above C.
        Placed on wall above fireplace L.2.
One telephone bell connected up to ring on stage
    up C.

One telephone bell connected up to ring on stage R.3. above door R.

(See that SOUND of bells differ. Buttons off R. for Stage Manager to ring.)

Electric push button L. of double doors.

Electric push bell button L. of double doors *(dead)*.

Enough cable to reach from *back of French windows* L.C. (Push button at window on floor outside set. Small lamp on cable. Off R.3.

Spot Light—For Flashlight Effect—well off R.*3*— to spot Man.

Foot of Stairs—In Alcove—about R.C.—Cue given twice. (Once in Act I, again in Act II.)

Small stand light off Right for Stage Manager. No bunches or strips used for any entrances throughout performance. All dark back of French windows. Off L.3, lamp for lightning, Act I and II.

On Set, Act I and II, stand lamp (connected), and to go out on separate cue in Act II. Up L.3 at window above door L.3.

Stand lamp on table C. Stand lamp on stand down R. below door R.2.

(To work with brackets. Stereopticon with glass slide of a bat to work across French windows Left to Right on cue.)

See Cue Sheet. For Company Electrician.

ACT III

Blue box lamp on window (on at opening).

Red box lamp on window work on cue.

Red spot lamp on window work on cue.

STAGE MANAGER NOTES

FOR ACT II

Note. Lights full up—Opening.

Prop. roll on floor, for Dale to hide blueprint in.
Prop. roll front of table Center.
Candles on table—not lighted—blow out after Act I.
Replace real phone up Center with rubber phone for
    fight. Doctor and Detective.
See that cigarette Dick puts on ashtray (Act I) is
    not removed.
See that piece of blueprint—in fender of grate—
    Fireplace.
Remove Dale's coat. Rubbers. Ouija Board. News-
    paper.
Note. For movement of characters in this act.
Switch armchair from L. of table to Left near fire-
    place.
Switch single chair from fireplace to L. of table C.
Sweep up glass broken, at French windows up L.C.
See that Key is in door. Up L.3.
See that writing paper and pencil are up stage stand
    above library table Center.

"THE BAT"

PUBLICITY THROUGH YOUR LOCAL PAPERS

The press can be an immense help in giving publicity to your productions. In that belief, we submit a number of suggested press notes which may be used either as they stand or changed to suit your own ideas and submitted to the local press.

SYNOPSIS

Cornelia Van Gorder, a maiden lady of sixty, rents the summer home of a New York banker who had been reported dead in Colorado some months before. She is warned that mysterious things are happening around the house, but she refuses to move. About this time it is discovered that a large sum of money is missing from the dead banker's bank. Immediately the suspicion is aroused that, far from being dead, he has stolen the money, hidden it in a secret chamber in his house, and is awaiting a good chance to sneak back and get it. Four different people are after the money—the bank cashier, wrongfully accused of taking it; a detective engaged by Miss Van Gorder to clear up the mystery; a doctor friend and supposed confederate of the missing banker, and The Bat, a notorious thief who has long eluded the police. There are mysterious murders, shivery rappings and many false leads for the audience to follow before the mystery is finally cleared.

PUBLICITY

Of all the mystery plays which have been produced on the American stage (and there are hundreds of them), "The Bat" has proven to be the daddy of them all. Incident is piled on incident with skill and plausibility, and it is impossible to know who the real criminal is until the final curtain.

This play is founded on Mary Roberts Rinehart's famous story, "The Circular Staircase," and the dramatization was made by Mrs. Rinehart and the late Avery Hopwood.

"The Bat" is a marked departure from that highly successful farce, "Seven Days," by these same authors, and it is a convincing proof of their high standing as dramatists that they were able to write successfully on such widely different themes.

In their endeavor to maintain the high standard they have set, the ————— Players have selected "The Bat" for their next production at the ————— Theatre on ————— evening.

The drama is being rehearsed with infinite care and enthusiasm and the performance will be calculated to raise this popular dramatic organization to even greater heights of public approval than it has hitherto enjoyed.

The mystery play has long been a favorite diversion for theatregoers all over the world. Every year brings forth its crop of new thrillers. But standing forth like a beacon in the history of the American stage is "The Bat," by Mary Roberts Rinehart and Avery Hopwood. No other play of thrills and mystery has ever surpassed this masterpiece and few have equalled it.

Time and again these two dramatists have proved themselves to be masters of their craft, and "The Bat" is the product of both at their best.

The skill and naturalness with which the accusing finger points from one character to the other as the real criminal keeps the audience on tenterhooks throughout the entire performance. This is one mystery drama where the truth does not come out until the very end of the play, and it is impossible to guess what the outcome is going to be or what will happen from one minute to the other.

But above all, the play is thoroughly believable at all times. There is no straining for effect, no false dramaturgy. The characters are all human, everyday people caught in a web of baffling occurrences.

"The Bat" will be presented for the edification of our local theatre lovers by the ————— Players at the ————— Theatre, on ————— evening. Come and shiver with your friends.

———————

Why do people love to be thrilled? Why have great men, from time immemorial, revelled in devouring stories of the hair-raising, blood-curdling type? It is a hard question to answer, but the average man seems to find increasing satisfaction in each new crop of gooseflesh he cultivates through the medium of the mystery story or play.

Perhaps it is because we never outgrow our childhood—when we told one another ghost stories in the attic or imagined the cellar to be the abode of gnomes, goblins or the bogey man himself.

When we get older we persist in our strange, wierd pastime, and although we know it is only a book or a play, we are thrilled just as in childhood. Imagination is indeed a persistent thing and few of us escape it.

Poe, Maupassant, Gaboriau, Stevenson, Doyle—all these noted authors have given us masterpieces which have thrilled the world and will continue to do so for many generations to come.

Among our contemporary writers of this type of story, Mary Roberts Rinehart stands at the head. For years she has supplied us with yarns that terrify and amuse. Among her happiest efforts stands "The Circular Staircase," on which that celebrated play, "The Bat," is founded. This play was written by Miss Rinehart in collaboration with the brilliant Avery Hopwood and proved to be the most successful mystery the American stage has ever known.

"The Bat" will be presented by the ——————— Players at the ——————— Theatre, on ——————— evening.

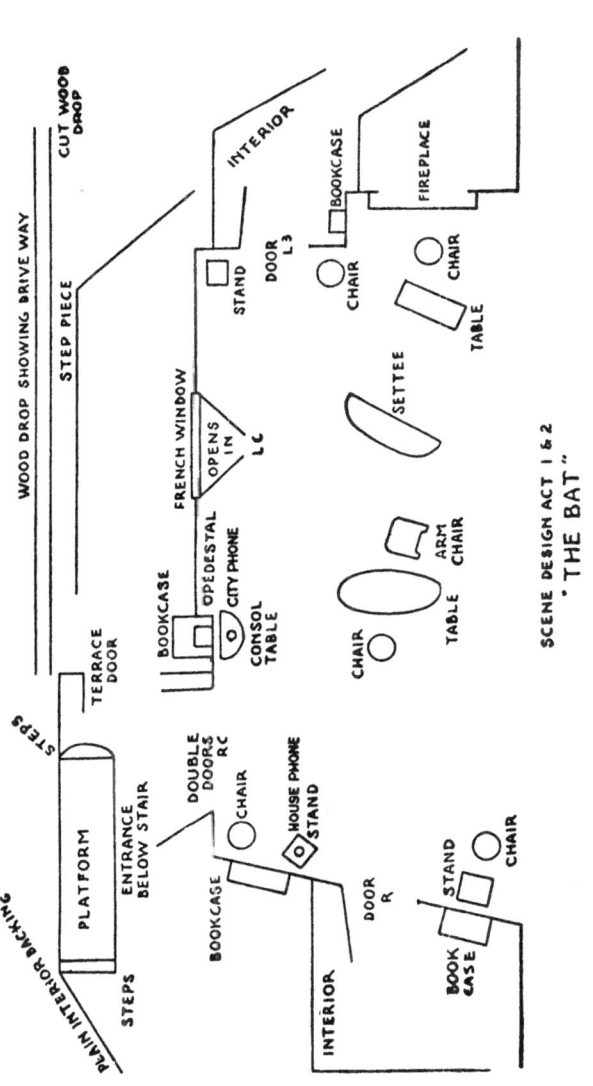

PLAN INTERIOR BACKING

WOOD DROP SHOWING DRIVE WAY

STEP PIECE

CUT WOOD DROP

INTERIOR

BOOKCASE

FIREPLACE

STAND

DOOR L 3

CHAIR

CHAIR

TABLE

FRENCH WINDOW

OPENS IN

L C

SETTEE

BOOKCASE

PEDESTAL

CITY PHONE

CONSOL TABLE

ARM CHAIR

CHAIR

TABLE

TERRACE DOOR

STEPS

PLATFORM

ENTRANCE BELOW STAIR

DOUBLE DOORS R C

CHAIR

HOUSE PHONE STAND

BOOKCASE

DOOR R

STAND

CHAIR

BOOK CASE

INTERIOR

STEPS

SCENE DESIGN ACT 1 & 2
" THE BAT "

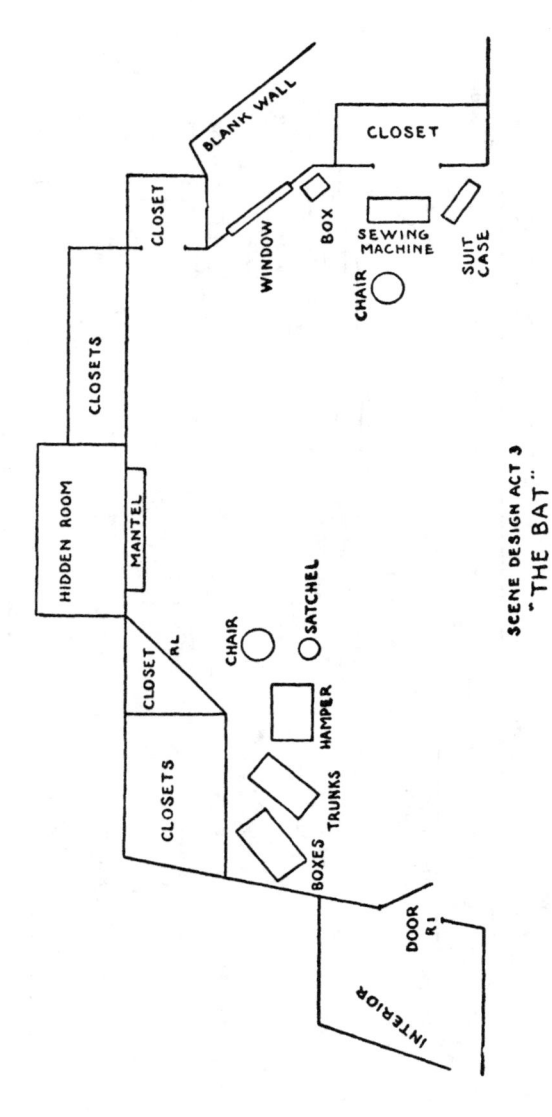

SCENE DESIGN ACT 3
"THE BAT"